DUDE MAGNET

THE LAST PICKS  BOOK 2

GREGORY ASHE

H&B

Dude Magnet

Copyright © 2024 Gregory Ashe

Published by Hodgkin & Blount
https://www.hodgkinandblount.com/
contact@hodgkinandblount.com

Published 2024
Printed in the United States of America

Version 1.05

Trade Paperback ISBN: 978-1-63621-082-7
eBook ISBN: 978-1-63621-081-0

CHAPTER 1

"I think we might possibly, maybe, have made a mistake," I said.

At the top of Hemlock House's grand staircase, the bride-to-be asked, "What about this ceiling? Could we smash it out?"

My friends looked to me for a response.

The Last Picks—they called themselves that because they were always the last picks in gym (and for pretty much everything else)—were here today because: a) they were almost always here, and b) they were providing emotional support, and c) this was all Millie's fault. (As a side note, I definitely fell into that "last picks" category too.) There were five of us: Millie, who was like a tiny blond version of a caffeinated Energizer bunny. Indira, with her laugh lines and that lone shock of white hair like a witch. Fox, their graying hair buzzed—today, under a top hat that featured little gears and welding goggles, and which didn't go with what they had told me (at length) was called a seductress blouse. And Keme, short and lean and tan from a summer of surfing, his long hair pushed behind his ears.

"Oh my God," Millie whisper-screamed. "They're so in love! Isn't this the cutest? This is the CUTEST!"

"Mom," the groom-to-be shouted down the stairs. "Can we do something about this ceiling?"

"The cutest," Fox murmured. They sounded like someone trying to pick out their favorite knife.

Keme didn't quite make a growling noise, but he folded his arms—audibly—and set his jaw as he stared at the happy couple.

"Tell them no." Indira nudged me. "Tell them they can't make any alterations."

"Why me?" I asked.

The groom's mother and father and grandmother were making their way up the stairs now: Mom on her phone. Dad panting. Grandma testing each step by hammering down with the ferrule of her cane.

"Because it's your house," Millie said unhelpfully.

"Because I already had to stop them with the wallpaper," Fox said with a definite tone.

Keme gave me a look that translated to: *Don't be such a wuss.*

"Because this was your idea," Indira said.

I gaped at them. "This was Millie's idea!"

Millie nodded enthusiastically and then said, "I bet her dress is going to be gorgeous."

There wasn't much doubt about that since the Gauthier-Meadows clan, who were currently occupying my grand staircase, had Scrooge McDuck kind of money. And I needed money. When I'd decided to stay in Hastings Rock, I'd been certain that I could make my savings stretch for a year. That seemed like a reasonable amount of time—a year to get settled, to really start writing. The thing about suddenly coming into possession of a Class V haunted mansion, though? (That's my personal ranking system, by the way.) They cost a lot of money. Buckets of money. Even when they're in great condition, like Hemlock House. And since I was still, uh, brainstorming my brilliant masterpiece of a novel that would doubtless bring me instant fame and fortune, and since I had no employable skills, I needed to do something. Also, in Millie's (and, I suppose, my) defense, the idea had sounded like a good one. Hemlock House—with its wainscoting and damask wallpaper and antique Chesterfields and curios and, most importantly, books—was beautiful. It was enormous. And it was one of those rare period homes that had survived into the twenty-first century relatively unscathed. Combined with the scenery of the Oregon Coast at its peak in early September, it was a picture-perfect place for a wedding. Or so Millie and I had claimed in the online ads.

We had not accounted for things like, I don't know, acoustics.

The bride-to-be tilted her head back and belted out a note.

Millie winced.

Keme covered his ears.

Fox said, "It's like someone stuffed a cat inside a set of bagpipes."

"It's a travesty," Indira said.

"It's the acoustics," the bride-to-be announced. "They're all wrong."

Even the groom-to-be looked like he was having a bit of trouble swallowing that explanation. A laugh from farther down the hall made me glance over. The groom-to-be's identical twin was leaning against a piece of gorgeous period furniture that Indira insisted on calling a commode. (I refused to call it that because, as far as I could tell, it was just a chest of drawers.) Next to him, the maid of honor (to be?) was covering a grin.

"Mom," the groom-to-be said. "The ceiling?"

"I'll call a contractor," she said without looking up from her phone.

Fox hissed.

Indira shoved me forward.

The sound of my steps must have drawn their attention, because every eye turned toward me. Mom even deigned to look up from her phone.

"Uh, you know," I said. "About the house."

"You can't rip out the ceiling," Fox prompted in a whisper.

"Why not?" the grandmother asked. "We'll pay for it."

"Well," I said.

Apparently, they wanted more than that.

The twin looked like he was trying not to laugh again.

"It's not so much the money," I said, "as it is that you, um, can't."

"What's he saying?" the bride-to-be asked. "I don't understand what he's saying."

"It's a historic house," I said. "And the contract clearly says no alterations."

"But the acoustics," the bride-to-be wailed. "My head. Baby, I'm getting a headache."

"Why's it such a big deal?" Dad asked. He was too loud, and it didn't go well with his rounded shoulders and potbelly. "It's a house. And we said we'd pay."

Mom gave him a freezing glance and said, "Get the contract, Gary."

Gary grimaced at her; it took me a moment to realize it was supposed to be a smile. He scurried down the steps, darted past us—with a glare for me—and disappeared outside. Behind him, he left a trail of crumbling dirt that his hiking boots—perfectly appropriate for a wedding rehearsal, right?—had quite literally tracked throughout the house.

"Sharian," Fox said, "why don't we talk about the reception? Millie, come on."

"And Mrs. Meadows," Indira said, "I wanted to go over a few of the dietary restrictions your guests noted."

The double distractions broke the tension of the moment. Sharian (the bride-to-be) dragged Mason (the groom-to-be) down the stairs, and they followed Fox and Millie into the living room. Indira moved to join Mom and Grandma, where they began to confer.

Keme hadn't abandoned me, although he was giving me a look that mingled disappointment and amusement.

"Fine," I said. "Next time, you can tell them."

He rolled his eyes and headed toward the kitchen.

"Hey."

The voice came from behind me, and I turned. It was the twin, Cole. He and his brother were unobjectionably handsome: dark hair, dark eyes, athletic builds even though they were going into their thirties. Mason (the groom-to-be) wore his hair in a side part with waves, and he looked every bit the high-achieving son of a fantabulously wealthy family, aside from a coconut-bead necklace—which felt like a lame bit of leftover teenagery. Cole (aka Trouble) wore a matching necklace, but he kept his hair shorter. It was hard to name a specific style since he looked like he'd just woken up. Under a bridge. After a seriously rough night. The joggers and hoodie weren't helping his case; they must have been expensive, but they looked lived-in, to put it generously.

"Hi," I said.

"You're cute." He leaned against a console table. It rocked, and a porcelain vase wobbled. Cole said a word you're not supposed to say in front of your grandma and caught the vase (barely). Then he looked at me.

"Excuse me," I said. "I've got to check on a few things."

Which was a total lie. But I did walk purposefully toward the den and open the door and stand there, hands on hips, pretending to scrutinize something. Through the window, I had a good line of sight to Gary (father-of-the-groom), who was currently vaping and playing a game on his phone. I thought it was a calculated risk; Becky (mother-of-the-groom) did not seem like the kind of woman who tolerated loafing around.

"Okay," Trouble (aka Cole) said behind me, "that was embarrassing."

Trying not to sigh, I turned around. Again.

"I was trying to look cool," he said with a grin.

"I liked the part at the end where you almost broke an irreplaceable vase."

His grin got bigger. "That wasn't my favorite part, actually."

"Uh huh."

"My favorite part was when I told you how cute you are."

I rolled my eyes. Loudly.

That made him burst out laughing. He stepped in, closing the distance between us, and all of a sudden Keme was there. Keme had to be five or six inches shorter than this guy, and although Keme was definitely stronger than he looked—cue one humiliating bout of Millie-inspired wrestling—he was still a

9

teenager (a teenager, it must be noted, who was perpetually hungry, ate everything Indira put in front of him, and still looked like he'd disappear if he turned sideways). Cole probably had thirty pounds on him, and those thirty pounds were muscle.

None of it slowed Keme down. He put himself between us, hand on Cole's chest, and shoved. Cole took a surprised step back and said, "Whoa."

Keme glowered at him.

"It's all right," I said, touching Keme's arm. The boy's whole body was tight with a kind of fight-or-flight energy; Keme was practically buzzing with it. I'd never seen him like this before. "It's okay," I said in a softer voice. "We were talking."

Keme shook his head at my words and then pointed to his eye and then to Cole. It was getting easier to understand Keme, although I still wished he'd talk (Indira insisted he was perfectly able to, but I'd never heard a word from him).

I tried to interpret his gesture. "You've got your eye on him—"

Keme shook his head and pointed to his eye again.

Then I saw it. "Oh. He's high."

Cole laughed and rubbed the back of his neck. "Not, like, super high. Just enough to float through this. Sorry, did I do something wrong?"

"No," I said. I squeezed Keme's arm and got him moving. "I'm sorry about the confusion. Are you okay?"

"Yeah, of course—"

"Great. Excuse us."

I steered Keme into what was called the north lobby (because in a place like Hemlock House, even weird little side pockets needed their own special names). Voice low, I asked, "What's going on?"

Keme wouldn't look at me.

"Hey. Mister."

Slowly, he dragged his eyes to my face. His arm was still tense under my hand. He set his jaw.

After a deep breath, I said, "Thank you."

A hint of confusion showed in his eyes.

"For caring," I said. "And for being worried."

He shrugged.

"But," I said.

He tried to pull free.

I held on. "But," I said again, "you can't go around pushing people and—"

Keme yanked his arm away and, before I could stop him, pushed through the door to the servants' dining room. A moment later, a second door slammed, and I knew he'd left Hemlock House in true teenager fashion.

"Everything okay?"

That was Trouble with a capital T again.

"Do you always sneak up behind people?" I asked.

The smile made him look younger. "I'm off my game today."

The maid of honor was watching us from down the hall, and she looked like she was enjoying every minute of this agony.

"Can we start over?" Cole asked.

"I don't have an unlimited supply of vases."

He grinned and said, "Hi, I'm Cole."

"You look familiar. I think I've seen you before."

"Nope, that was my twin. I'm way better looking."

"Uh huh."

"It's easy to tell us apart. For example, I'm a lefty. I know for a fact that Taylor Swift is a million times better than Beyonce, I've got way better handwriting, I never wear red because that was the only color my mom let me wear when I was growing up, and Mason is a total lightweight when it comes to, uh, certain substances."

"You're losing me," I told him.

"I've definitely got a better sense of humor, I'm not a corporate sellout, oh, yeah, and I've got these little freckles in a certain spot." He gave me the grin again. "But I need to know you a little better before I show you."

"Cute."

"See? I think you're cute. You think I'm cute. We're a match."

In spite of myself, I laughed. "Let's keep this strictly professional."

"God, no. That sounds terrible. Can I take you to dinner?"

I made a noise and slid around him.

Cole moved with me, stepping into my path. "Please let me take you to dinner."

"I've got to work."

"We can go whenever you're done. I'm a bum and a loser, to quote my parents, so I'm at your beck and call."

"There's a million things to do before the wedding."

"But you have to eat sometime, right? What if I pick up food and bring it over?"

I tried to slide around him again.

He moved with me again. "Please? It's dinner. I'll be a perfect gentleman." He held up two fingers. "I won't even get high."

"I think the Scouts do three fingers."

"But you knew what I was going for! See how in sync we are?"

That made me laugh again.

I almost said no. But he had a great smile: big and bright and wide. And I'd always liked confident guys. And, if I had a gun to my head, I could admit I was, well, lonely.

Not *lonely* lonely. I mean, I had Millie and Fox and Indira and Keme—they were the best thing to happen to me in a long time. They were my friends. We were the Last Picks, and I loved spending time with them. But friends or no friends, the transition from a long-term, serious relationship to being totally, absolutely, unrelentingly single hadn't been easy. I missed quiet nights staying in with my person. I missed the easiness of casual touch. I missed intimacy—not sex, but, yeah, that too. And while I wasn't under any delusions that Mr. Trouble with a capital T was going to be my one true love, he seemed sweet and fun and unexpectedly earnest. He'd already made me laugh twice; that was a good sign, right?

"What are your parents going to say?"

"Oh God, they've known we're bi for, like, ever."

That wasn't what I'd expected, but it was an interesting tidbit nevertheless. "Not what I meant."

"If I skip all the pre-wedding festivities? I'm a constant disappointment. They'd be worried if I didn't screw things up."

"That's not as encouraging as you think."

"I feel like you're about to say yes."

"Dinner," I said.

His grin lit up his face.

I held up a finger. "Only dinner."

"I told you: I'm a perfect gentleman."

"Who's also a perpetual disappointment."

"Well, yeah," he said. He had a dimple, I realized. An extremely dangerous dimple. "Have you met my family? So, if I could get your number…"

As I finished rattling off digits, raised voices erupted in the living room. Cole's expression changed to resignation, and I slipped past him (successfully, this time) to return to the hall.

The pocket doors to the living room were open, and the family was clustered around Mason (the groom-to-be) in a shouting scrum: Becky (Mom), Gary (Dad), Sharian (the bride-to-be), and Jodi (Grandma).

"What are you talking about?" Gary boomed. "You're out of your mind."

Becky said something that, once you cleaned it up, was something along the lines of "Are you an idiot?"

Sharian was wailing, "I don't understand. I don't understand."

"It's my money," Mason said. "That's what the trust says. It's mine once I turn thirty-one. I can do whatever I want with it."

"But I don't understand," Sharian said. "My head. Oh my God, my head, I'm going to be sick."

"There's nothing to understand," Mason said. "I'm giving it away to charity. All of it. End of conversation. It's mine, and I can do whatever I want—"

Mason's grandmother slapped him. The crack of the blow silenced everyone. Mason shook his head; to judge by the look in his eyes, he'd never been hit before. The grandmother raised her hand like she might hit him again, but instead, she spoke, her voice low and controlled and furious. "It is my money, you stupid, selfish boy."

No one said anything for what felt like a long time. No one moved. No one breathed.

"I'm going to be sick," Sharian moaned again. She took a tottering step. "Penny? Where's Penny?"

That was when I noticed the maid of honor was missing.

Next to me, Cole let out a harsh breath. His cheeks were flushed, and his hands were trembling; he tried hiding them in his pockets, but the first time, he couldn't get them in. He didn't even seem to realize I was still there as he said to himself, "Mase, you moron."

I needed to say something. I needed to suggest we take a break. Maybe everyone needed some space.

But as I opened my mouth, something impossible happened.

A man walked into the hall. He looked impeccably handsome: square jawed, swooshy haired, that strong nose that he didn't like, but that was, of course, perfect for his face. Cardigan and chinos and boat shoes. He looked like he'd fallen out of a different time, a different place—somewhere, undoubtedly, with a lot more money.

He glanced around the hall, confusion scrawled across those yacht club features, and then his eyes settled on me. The old, familiar smile spread across his face, and for a moment, I forgot how it had ended.

"Dash!" he called out.

"Uh, hi, Hugo."

CHAPTER 2

Technically, it's not pure and total cowardice if you run away for a good reason. At least, that's what I chose to tell myself.

After mumbling something that might have passed for human speech, I fled—er, escaped—er, dashed (oh my God) into the servants' dining room.

My first clear thought was: He's going to yell at me.

A full-body flush prickled through me. My eyes stung. I tried to remember how to breathe. Slowly, bit by bit, I took control of myself again. I focused on the gingham curtains. I looked out the windows onto the sea cliffs and, below, the rollers coming in.

Hugo was here.

Hugo was in Hastings Rock.

Hugo was in Hemlock House.

Hugo was in my hall, looking impossibly Hugo-ish.

For someone who had spent a lifetime perfecting the fine art of avoiding confrontation, conflict, and any version of addressing his problems in a head-on and adult manner, this was an unmitigated disaster.

The door opened behind me, and I whirled around.

Indira, Millie, Keme, and Fox filed into the room. Indira gave me a worried look. Fox frowned. Keme's face was dour. And Millie darted forward to give me a hug.

"Are you okay?" she whispered.

"Yeah." I wiped my eyes and cleared my throat. "Yeah, I'm fine."

"Oh Dash," she said and squeezed me harder.

When Millie had finished demolishing my ribcage, we sat at the table, where Indira, Fox, and Keme had already taken chairs. Keme kept shooting dark looks at the door as though he expected to have to launch to his feet at any moment. Indira was watching me with dark eyes. Fox played with what looked like an engineer's pocket watch that had somehow been turned into a brooch.

"So," Fox said. "That was Hugo."

I nodded.

"Should I call Bobby?" Millie asked.

"What?" The thought of Deputy Bobby—of confident, strong, *direct* Deputy Bobby, with his burnished bronze eyes that didn't miss anything—meeting Hugo made me sit up in my chair. "Oh my God, no!"

"But if he's dangerous—"

"Hugo's not dangerous," I said. "He's—Hugo." I heard how that sounded and added, "He's not supposed to be here, that's all. He caught me off guard."

That was putting it mildly. A few months ago, Hugo and I had been dating. More than dating, actually. We'd been living together. And Hugo had been planning on proposing. Which was all well and good, except I didn't love Hugo. And so we'd broken up, and I'd moved across the country. And now, out of the blue, here he was.

"He's in my house," I moaned and clutched my hair.

"That does seem to be the case," Fox said.

My head came up. "My parents!"

"Your parents are coming?" Indira asked.

"No! He's going to tell them!"

"Tell them what?" Fox asked.

"Everything!"

Even Millie's eyes got a little wide at that.

"Dash," Indira said, "take a deep breath. I understand it's a bit of a surprise, but I thought you ended things on amicable terms."

"We did," I groaned. "You don't understand. He's going to be so...Hugo-ish about this. That's why he's here. It's going to be a disaster. It's going to be one of those train wrecks that keeps going and going."

"Maybe he's here on vacation," Millie said.

I gave her a look, but because she was Millie, she beamed at me.

"I know it's not always comfortable," Fox said, "bumping into an ex. And I'm sure you have a lot of feelings about...about how things ended. But Dash, you didn't do anything wrong." Their voice softened as they reached across the table to squeeze my hand. "You don't need to feel embarrassed or ashamed or defensive. His feelings aren't your responsibility. You have to take care of yourself."

I nodded. "You're right."

Fox's eyes narrowed.

"You're absolutely right."

"No," they said. "We are not burning Hemlock House down and faking your death."

"It's the only way," I said. "You don't know how Hugo is. He'll keep coming and coming."

"Like the Terminator," Millie said brightly.

"Oh my God, the Gauthier-Meadowses! Are they still—"

"They're gone." Fox waved a hand. "And you're stalling."

"I'm not stalling. I'm actively pursuing a new and interesting topic."

"This is silly," Indira said. "Go tell him that you'd like him to leave, and that'll be the end of it."

I gaped at her.

"I changed my mind," Fox said. "I'm on board with burning down the house."

"Thank you," I said.

"Dashiell, stop it." Indira's voice was flat. "Fox, don't encourage him. Tell him to go away, and I'll make us a cake for tonight."

"You can't bribe me into being a responsible, mature, problem-solving adult. I'm going to run away, like Fox said." Inspiration struck. "I'm going to join the circus."

"It'll be a *tres leches* cake."

A little too quickly, I said, "I suppose I could at least hear what he has to say."

Keme gave me a look of undiluted disgust.

"This is how adults handle their problems," I told him loftily.

"You're going the wrong way," Millie said with unnecessary enthusiasm.

I ignored her as I tried to get the back door open. "I didn't say I was going to talk to him right now."

Keme rubbed his face.

"Dashiell," Indira said.

"I'm not saying I want you to burn Hemlock House down and make everyone believe I perished in a record-breaking inferno—"

"I know this is going to sound crazy," Fox said, "but I'm even more invested in this plan when he says it like that."

"—but I wouldn't be angry if you did."

"You cannot run away from your problems forever," Indira said.

Shows what you know, I thought as I pulled the door shut behind me. The late summer day was warm and smelled like the briny, ocean winds and the dusty hemlocks that gave the house its name. I had been successfully running away from my problems since March 16th, 1990—

As I came around the side of the house, I crashed into Hugo.

We both fell, but Hugo picked himself up first. Then he helped me up. He dusted me off, and, rubbing his head where we'd collided, he gave a rueful smile.

"You were waiting for me?" I demanded, rubbing my own goose egg.

"Hello, Dash. For the second time."

"Hi. For the second time. And now goodbye. For the first time."

I tried to step around him, but Hugo held out a hand. He didn't grab me. He didn't even move into my path the way Cole had. But I stopped.

"I know this is uncomfortable for you," he said. "I know that I'm asking you to do something difficult for you. But I'd like to have a conversation with you about our relationship—"

"We're not in a relationship. We broke up."

Hugo took a deep breath. "I didn't get the closure I needed from that conversation. And, if I'm being honest, I think you broke up with me because you were scared. I think that's a bad reason to throw something wonderful away."

"Well—" The best I could come up with was "Too bad. I'm sorry you didn't get closure, but we already had this conversation—"

"You told me you wanted to break up," Hugo said, "and you left the next morning. You won't answer my calls. You won't respond to my messages. Dottie's worried sick about you, you know."

That comment from my sister felt like a low blow, particularly since she'd been too busy backpacking through—God, I thought maybe she was in Vietnam right now—to do more than send the occasional text.

Hugo continued, "If your parents hadn't told me where you were and what you were doing, I would have thought you were dead." A tiny quaver worked its way into his voice as he asked, "Do you know what that felt like?"

A gull flapped into view and then banked sharply. Its cry seemed like it came from a long way off.

"I'm sorry," I said in a small voice.

He nodded. His eyes looked full, and he blinked a few times. "I know. And I understand that—that you have a pattern of dealing with problems this way. But I don't think it was fair to me. And I don't think it's fair to us, Dash. I love you. And I know you love me. If there are problems, then let's talk about them. Let's see a counselor. Let's work on them together." He caught my hand, and I still remembered how it felt, to have his fingers wrapped around mine. "I never should have let you go. I should have said all of this when you told me you wanted to leave. But I…I couldn't believe what was happening. I couldn't think. I did everything wrong. And so I'm here, now, and I'm trying to do it right."

It took me a moment to work up the courage. "Hugo, I'm sorry I hurt you. I am. And I'm sorry I left, well, abruptly. But I'm not sorry we broke up. And I don't want to get back together."

He nodded. "I think we should see a therapist."

"Uh, no."

"We need to see one, Dash. Together. We can do it out here, if that will make you more comfortable."

"Hugo, I don't think you're listening to me."

"I'm listening to you. But Dash, this is the exact same thing all over again. You don't want to deal with your problems. You don't want to have hard conversations. For heaven's sake, you tried to sneak out the back door so you wouldn't have to talk to me."

"And I stand by that plan."

"You don't think you love me." Hugo shrugged. "Okay. But let's talk to a therapist about what that means in terms of your inability to make decisions, your conflict avoidance, your perfectionism, your unwillingness to be vulnerable and intimate—"

I yanked my hand away.

"That's not how I meant it," Hugo said hurriedly.

"Please go home, Hugo. I don't want to see you again."

"I'm not giving up on us." Hugo raised his chin. "I've been reading Brené Brown. I'm daring greatly. I'm being brave for the sake of our love."

I turned and headed back toward Hemlock House.

"You can tell yourself that it was me," Hugo called after me. "You can tell yourself I was the problem, that you didn't love me, that everything will be okay when you find the right guy. But you're lying to yourself, Dash. The only thing standing in the way of your happiness is you."

CHAPTER 3

I was going to kill Hugo, I decided that afternoon.

How's that for an inability to make decisions?

I was going to kill him. I was going to murder him. I was going to…kill him.

Ease up on the judgment, please. My internal thesaurus doesn't work when I'm stressed.

I spent the afternoon telling anyone who would listen about my concrete, set-in-stone, uh, concrete plans. I was going to kill Hugo. And when I wasn't telling them about killing Hugo, I told them how wrong he was.

"So, I worry about details," I told Fox. "So, I care about the little things."

"Not your clothes," Fox said.

"I'm talking about—"

"Not your physical health. Not your conditioning. Not décor. Not—"

"I'm talking about my writing!"

"Next time, yell in this ear," Fox said. "To even out the deafness."

Millie was a much better listener.

"I don't have a fear of being vulnerable."

"Oh no, definitely not."

"I'm willing to make myself vulnerable."

She nodded enthusiastically.

"I'd love to have a strong emotional bond with a partner."

"Like Bobby."

That threw me for a second. "I guess so. I mean, Deputy Bobby and West are a great couple—"

"No, no, no. You and Bobby. Like, when you had that fight with your mom, you told him all about it, and he listened and nodded and gave you good advice. Or when you got that story back, and you were so upset that you told Indira you were only going to eat soup, even though you hate soup—"

"It's a drink! It's not a meal!"

"—and Bobby came, and five minutes later you were laughing, and I swear you smiled for a week."

"Well, that's not—"

"And that time you got homesick, and Bobby made you go on a run with him, and you came back, like, super sweaty, and Fox thought you were having a heart attack—"

"It was his eyes," Fox called from the next room. "They were bulgy."

"My eyes were fine!" I snapped.

"—and after the run you told Bobby all about how you were feeling, and he did such a good job listening, and then you were better." Millie straightened up with a fresh burst of perkiness. "You're very good at emotional intimacy!"

"I have to talk to someone else," I said.

Indira was baking in the kitchen (living up to her promise of a *tres leches* cake, although I think it was more out of pity than because I'd actually earned it).

"And if I'm so bad at making decisions, why did I pack up my whole life and move out here, huh? What about that?"

"I know, dear," Indira said. "Do you want some more coffee?"

"I don't know."

She went back to measuring.

"It's a little late," I said.

She made a noise that I guessed was supposed to mean she'd heard me.

"But also, I'm supposed to go out with Cole, so maybe I do need a pick-me-up."

"Mm-hmm."

"Maybe with a little cream and sugar."

"In the fridge, dear."

"But Fox did say something about my figure. Should I call it my figure? Does that have a misogynistic connotation?"

All that earned me was a "Uh-huh."

"How much coffee are you supposed to drink in one day? Can you drink too much coffee? Can it make you sick?"

Indira must not have heard me because she looked intent on her mixing.

"Maybe tea," I said. "Or is tea worse for you?"

"Dashiell?"

"Yes?"

"Please get out of my kitchen."

Keme was playing video games in the billiards room. Today, it was one of the *Resident Evil* games, which were way, way, way too scary (for me, not for Keme).

After explaining everything to Keme—at length—I said, "And he's not even being consistent." I laughed. "That's what's so funny about this whole thing." I laughed again. "He's contradicting himself, right?"

Keme was trying to kill—well, I wasn't sure what it was. Either a Depression-era public works employee who was building a trail, or, uh, a zombie (also building a trail). Maybe I'd forgotten what these games were about.

"Because I'm not conflict avoidant."

Keme switched to a different gun. He seemed to be squeezing the buttons on the controller extra hard.

"I didn't avoid conflict when I told him I wanted to break up, did I?"

The public works zombie must have gotten the better of Keme because the screen went dark, and Keme let out a frustrated noise.

"I initiated the conflict," I said. "I'm pro-conflict. Well, not pro-conflict, God, I hope not. Am I pro-conflict?"

Keme held up a finger.

Maybe this was it. Maybe he was going to say something. Maybe the first words I ever heard from him were going to be how much he cared about me, and how I was a great guy, and I was so much better off without Hugo, and I'd totally made the right decision to break up with him.

Then Keme fished out a pair of earbuds, put them in his ears (firmly, I noticed), and resumed gameplay.

I slunk upstairs and took a long, prune-ifying bath.

A knock at the door interrupted my plan to slowly dissolve into human soup.

"It's almost time for your date!" Millie squealed. "Hurry up! We need to get ready!"

"I'm not going." And then, because I felt like I was on to something, "I'm going to die in the bath and dissolve into human soup."

"You hate soup," Millie reminded me.

"Where are your girdles?" Fox asked. "I can't find any."

"I don't have any girdles."

"Really? Then why does your stomach sometimes look—"

Another, louder rap covered up the rest of that unfortunate sentence. "Dashiell," Indira said, "get out of the bath."

"I can't. My arms already dissolved."

"I'll send Keme in."

"To drown me?"

Keme's exasperated huff was audible even through the door.

"If you're not out of there in the next minute," Indira said, "the kitchen is going gluten free."

For a moment, I froze. "You wouldn't dare."

"I have so many cookbooks, Dashiell. And I love a challenge."

The bathwater was getting cold. And I did hate soup.

Wrapped in a towel, I stood near the door and said, "All of you weirdos get out of my room!"

"We picked out your clothes," Millie said.

Fox said, "And your belt."

"Fox," Indira said.

"It's a precaution!"

"Why do I have to live like this?" I asked. "Why can't I have the kind of friends who convince me to do drugs and get tattoos and spend all my allowance on penny whistles?"

"Do you know what he reminds me of? What's that movie where a crotchety old lady body-swaps with a young man in the prime of his life?"

"All right," Indira said. "That's it. Everybody out."

The sounds of movement came, and then the door closed.

I let myself into the bedroom, half-braced for a Millie-related surprise. There wasn't a mean bone in Millie's body, but her...exuberance led to a lot of enthusiastic misunderstandings. Fortunately, I was alone, and I padded over to my bed to examine the clothes they'd laid out for me: a quilted jacket, lightweight enough that it'd be perfect once the sun went down; a chambray button-up; and black jeans. Apparently, I was authorized to choose my own underwear.

As I dressed, the reality of my situation began to settle in. Until now, the confrontation with Hugo had occupied my thoughts. But the fact was, I was going to dinner. With a guy. On what was, by any legal standard, a date. With Mr. Cole Meadows, who had dimples and looked like he swam or played rugby or lifted lots of heavy things (at least, when he wasn't high). And I was supposed to be funny. And charming. And smart.

And I was trying to put both legs through the same leg-hole.

"Hurry up," Fox said.

"I thought you left!"

"We did leave," Millie said, in the tone of someone who clearly thought they were being helpful. "Now we're waiting in the hall."

"Quit stalling," Fox said.

"I'm not stalling!" But I did have both legs in the same leg-hole. "I changed my mind. I'm not going."

"Indira has a key, remember?"

"I'm not scared of Indira."

That was a lie.

"You don't have to be scared of me," Indira said. "I'll send in Keme."

I finally got my legs in the right leg-holes, yanked the jeans up, and threw open the door. "I'm not scared of Keme either."

Keme folded his arms. And then, to make his point, he rolled his eyes.

"Oh my God," Millie said. "You look AMAZING!"

There's this deep-sea phenomenon called sonic tunnels—bands of water with exactly the right qualities to carry the sounds of undersea volcanoes across immense distances. I only mention it in case you need a point of comparison.

I was still working a finger in my ear as Indira said, "You look handsome, dear. Have a wonderful time on your date."

"Or have a terrible time," Fox said, "because I'm having a hard time picturing millennial-stoner bro-trust fund baby as your type."

"Fox," Indira said.

"What? I'm questioning his judgment. Out loud."

I sighed and looked at Keme. Apparently, he'd gotten over his anger or frustration or whatever it was because he offered a small smile and then pretended to blow his brains out.

"Yes," I said, "exactly. Finally, someone who gets it."

CHAPTER 4

The Otter Slide was the closest thing Hastings Rock had to a gay bar. It drew a younger, friendlier crowd than some of the other bars in town, and it was mostly a place for locals—it wasn't on the tourist strip, and on the outside, it wasn't quaint or cute or trendy. It was a single-story building with a built-up roof and shiplap siding. The large front windows were blacked out, and beer ads papered the walls.

What the outside lacked, though, the inside made up for with a kind of welcoming coziness. Pendant lights with green-and-gold glass were easy on the eyes, and a pool table and a *Star Wars* pinball machine gave you something to do (besides drinking) if you wanted to hang out with friends. The air smelled like hops and onion rings. (That's what heaven smells like, by the way.) Seely, the owner, still spent most nights behind the stick, and she made some of the best cocktails I'd ever had. She had a thing for little stuffed animals, and they were all over the bar: a little gay goat on the jukebox, a little gay bear in a bowl of bar mix, a nonbinary unicorn on a booth divider. A gorilla who was trying way too hard to give off daddy vibes perched on the pinball machine.

Over the last couple of months, this had become one of my favorite places to go with Indira, Fox, Millie, and Keme—although Keme had to be out by ten because he was a minor. I'd also spent a fair number of nights here with Deputy Bobby and his boyfriend, West. West, in particular, seemed to have decided that it was their responsibility as "local gays" (his words) to make sure I had plenty of opportunities to drink way too much and have cute boys pointed out to me.

Deputy Bobby and West were here tonight; I spotted them as soon as I stepped inside. West was beautiful—that was the only word for him. Pink cheeks, pouty lips, flaxen hair in a disheveled side part. And Deputy Bobby was literally what every guy was looking for. Objectively, I mean. Like, objectively, he had a face. And arms. And a butt. They were dancing on the little parquet dance floor at the back of the bar with a handful of other couples. Deputy Bobby had a beer in one hand (it would be a Rock Top, whatever their seasonal lager was), and his other hand held West close against him. Like, close. Like, cover the kids' eyes at the movies.

"Hey." A boozy breath on the side of my face made me turn. "You came."

Cole wore the same hoodie and joggers and coconut-bead necklace he'd had on earlier. His hair was still a mess. And his eyes were red and glassy.

"Hey," I said. And then I frowned. "You told me you weren't going to be messed up."

He gave me a rueful smile. It was a strangely vulnerable expression, with an unexpected amount of self-disgust.

"I think I'm going to go," I said.

"No, please." He caught my wrist, and his hand was warm and soft. "Please don't go. I'm sorry." He ran his thumb over the inside of my wrist. "It's been such an awful day, and looking forward to this has been the only thing that's kept me from going crazy."

I don't know what made me look past Cole, but my eyes went to Deputy Bobby again. He was still dancing with West, but he was staring at me, and I couldn't make sense of the expression on his face. It almost looked like he was angry, and Deputy Bobby never got angry. It did something to my stomach, this weird, flipping thing, and before I realized I was going to say it, I heard the words coming out of my mouth: "We can start with one drink."

Cole's smile broadened, and he ran his thumb along the inside of my wrist again.

After asking me what I wanted, he sat me in an empty booth and went to the bar. He came back again almost immediately. Seely was looking over, a question in her eyes; I nodded, and she went back to mixing drinks.

"Are those peaches?" Cole asked as he set my drink in front of me. "And cherries?"

"It's a house specialty, the summer Old Fashioned. Local produce." I took a drink to brace myself and asked, "Want to try?"

He did. He had a nice mouth, part of that unobjectionably handsome thing he had going on, and I thought about the cold glass against his lips.

"It's good," he said when he passed it back.

"Rock Top?" I asked, glancing at the brown bottle in his hand.

"It's all I drink when I'm here. They're so good; I don't know why they don't have better distribution."

"Maybe it's a good thing," I said.

"It's one of my two favorite things about Hastings Rock," he said as he looked me in the eye.

"I bet you say that to all the guys whose house you rent for a wedding."

"Definitely not." He let that land with some more eye contact.

Something was starting to build in his silence, a kind of charge to the conversation, so I blurted, "So, you and your family come here a lot?"

For a moment, I thought he was going to try to steer the conversation back to Intense Flirting (Hardcore Edition), but instead he relaxed into a smile. "Every year. Grandma loves this place, which means it's a mandatory vacation." He looked around. "I loved it when I was a kid, you know? Now it's one more family thing I have to do." I wanted to ask what that meant, but before I could, he said, "I'm sorry for, uh, showing up like this. I wanted to say that again. This afternoon—I mean, it was rough."

"I understand."

"Yeah?" His grin showed that strange self-dislike again. "I don't. God, they were all going at each other. Mom and Dad and Grandma going after Mason about—about that stupid thing with the money. Sharian and my parents. Sharian and Penny, even." I'd forgotten about the maid of honor, and it took me a moment to remember who he was talking about. "I've never seen Mason and Sharian fight like that. They called off the wedding; I don't know if they already told you. Big deal, right? I mean, they've only canceled it ten other times. But this time it felt real." Awareness penetrated some of the fog in his eyes, and he tried to smile again. He reached across the table to wrap his hand around mine. "I'm happy I'm here with you."

I fought the urge to pull my hand away and said, "Thanks."

Another of those silences came. It was strange, against the background of voices and bottles clinking and music. The song was Sia, "Cheap Thrills."

"So," Cole said, "how does a guy like you end up here?"

"Maybe I'm a local."

He burst out laughing.

"Hey," I said. "That's kind of rude."

For some reason, that only made him laugh harder. He still had his hand wrapped around mine. I was aware of people passing our booth, of the fact that they couldn't miss the physical contact. Hastings Rock was a small town, and it was even smaller when you removed the tourists from the equation. Gossip traveled fast. I thought of Deputy Bobby's face, the hard blankness of his expression earlier.

"Let me guess," he said. "You're on the run."

I made a buzzer noise.

"You're a movie star researching a role."

This time, I rolled my eyes.

"You've got to help me out," he said. "You're too cute and too smart; there's got to be a reason you're here."

"You didn't hear about Vivienne?"

"She's the writer, the one who used to live at that house. I thought she went to prison."

"Uh, yeah." I rolled my eyes again. "The short version is I came here for a job. It didn't work out, but I decided to stay."

"Oh yeah? And?"

"And what?"

"Do you like it?"

I shrugged. "For the most part. I mean, I think for a lot of people, I'm always going to be an outsider—maybe my great-great-great-grandchildren will eventually be considered locals."

"So," Cole said with a smirk. "You want kids."

"The jury's still out."

"Aren't you bored?"

"Without kids? No, trust me, I'm enough of a mess all by myself." I took a drink. "You mean here in Hastings Rock, I guess. No, not at all. It's beautiful. I love hiking. Well, maybe not hiking, but I love being outside in nature. I grew up in Portsmouth, so it's nice being by the water. And Hemlock House is amazing."

All he said was "Huh."

He brought the bottle to his lips. He really did have a nice mouth, and he caught me looking now and smiled around the brown glass. I could feel another of those frontal assaults coming: the high-octane flirting that was a kind of demand, asking me to—what? Well, I thought I had an idea, and it made me unwrap and re-wrap my hand around my glass.

Before he could get started, I said, "I guess I'm lonely. A little. Sometimes."

In the wake of my own words, I decided the only merciful thing at this point would be to drag my sorry butt out behind the Otter Slide and put me down gently.

But Cole's eyebrows knitted together, and he blinked. "Uh, yeah. I get that." He must have seen the confusion in my face because he gave a broken little laugh. "Come on, man. You want to talk about being a mess? I'm thirty, I've got no life, no friends. I'm hanging out in a bar in Hastings Rock."

"Gee, thanks."

"No, God." He made a frustrated noise. "I'm sorry, that's not what I meant. But, like, guys my age, they have their lives together. They have jobs. They have their own families. And I'm still getting dragged around by my grandma, going on vacation wherever she says we're going. Ten years ago, it was whatever. Now, what do I do? If Mom gives me my allowance, I go out and blow it. There are plenty of people who will be your friend as long as you're buying drinks. Then I'm broke, and you know what? People aren't so friendly. They're all younger. They have jobs. They go to school. God, do you know what it's like, partying with twenty-year-olds? It's terrible, man. I don't even know what a meme is."

That jarred a laugh loose from me.

Cole offered that stunner smile again. "You've got a nice laugh. You're way too good for me, just so you know. I'm telling you because I'm a little bit too high and because you're sweet: you should run away."

"If you don't like your life," I said, "why don't you change it? I know it's easier said than done, but you've got resources, right? You could go to school if you wanted a degree. If not, I bet your parents would help you get started in another business or trade."

He made a small, nasty noise that I realized, a beat later, was a *ha*. "You don't know my parents. They wanted two Masons: perfect little toys that would do whatever they wanted. If I want to go to college, I have to do a business degree or a law degree or an accounting degree, so I can work in the family business. If I want a job, I have to work in the family business."

"You don't have to ask your family for everything. You're friendly and polite. I'm sure you could get an entry-level job and start building your work experience. Or take out loans for school—"

He spoke as though he hadn't heard me. His voice was thicker, and I wondered how much he'd already had to drink (or smoke); it sounded like it was starting to hit him now. "Everything they wanted, Mason did. And look how messed up he is. He's getting married because he thinks he has to; he doesn't even know if he loves her, but he's going to marry her anyway. They'll probably be together forever too, like Mom and Dad." Cole stopped, and his throat worked, and he rubbed red-rimmed eyes. "I know I shouldn't be happy about what happened today. I know I shouldn't—I shouldn't be happy. But it's been so many years, my whole life, of hearing how perfect Mason is, and being compared to him, and being told what a screw-up I am. God, did you see their faces when he told them what he was going to do with that stupid money? They were so freaking mad."

The words sounded thrilled, almost gleeful, but I remembered how, when Mason had made his announcement, Cole had curled his hands into fists. How he had stared at his brother.

"Do you mind if I—" Cole slid out of the booth, patting himself down, and mumbled, "I'll be right back."

That, I decided, was my cue to call it a night. I checked with Seely to make sure he'd paid for our drinks, ignored the questioning look in her eye, and headed for the door. Sneaking out on people during a date wasn't exactly the best behavior, but neither was going to the restroom to get high.

I was only halfway across the bar when the door swung open, and two men stepped inside. They were making out furiously, hands and lips and tongues everywhere. A wave of confusion rolled over me because one of them was Cole. It took a moment before I realized that I was looking at Mason—the longer, side-part waves were one giveaway, and the different clothes helped too. The other guy had a strong, lean build, and beautiful dark hair, and yes, a cute butt—

A familiar butt.

"Hugo?" I said his name out loud without meaning to, but it didn't matter; the swell of music and voices covered it up.

It was definitely Hugo, and he was tongue-wrestling with Mason like his life was on the line. If the groom-to-be (I guess, ex-groom-to-be) had any reservations, it was hard to tell—he was currently trying to pull Hugo's shirt off.

When my brain rebooted, I had a single, panicked thought: get out. I glanced around, trying to find anything—a fire exit, a cat flap, an enchanted wardrobe to Narnia. Then Mason shouted, and I turned toward the noise.

He and Hugo had separated. Hugo slumped against the wall; he looked drunker than I'd ever seen him, and I was amazed he was still (semi) upright. Mason had a hand to his cheek; something red glistened beneath his fingers. Blood.

The woman who stood in front of Mason, fingers still curled into claws, was short and full bodied, with long, dark hair and first-class makeup. Penny, the maid of honor, held up her hands like she might try to tear Mason's face off again, and she shouted a stream of words that are not fit for TV before the 9pm watershed. Everyone in the bar had stopped their conversations; the only sound now came from the music—somebody had put on "Call Me Maybe."

Cole stumbled through a press of bodies and stared at the scene that was still unfolding. He looked, if anything, even more stoned, and his voice had a grating slowness as he stared at his brother and Hugo and Penny and said, "What's going on?"

Penny issued a final stream of invective, pushed past Hugo, and disappeared outside. Hugo looked like he was still standing only by the grace of God; his eyes were trying to roll up in his head. Mason grabbed napkins and held them to his bleeding cheek, and red seeped through the paper.

Cole was still staring. "What's wrong with you? Why do you have to ruin everything?"

Mason said some of those post-watershed words. Cole said some back. Mason said some more. Cole said a few new ones. And then they launched themselves at each other. They crashed into a table and flipped it. It crashed to the floor. Glasses and bottles shattered. Someone screamed. The brothers rolled across the vinyl flooring, hammering at each other. It didn't look like a scuffle. It didn't even look like a brawl. It looked like two guys trying to kill each other, only they were too far gone to make much progress at it.

I started forward—I wasn't sure what I was going to do, but somebody had to separate them. Before I could reach them, though, Deputy Bobby was there. He got Cole by the collar, and with seemingly no effort at all, heaved him up and off Mason. He shoved Cole toward me, and when Cole stumbled, I steadied him. Deputy Bobby picked Mason up and said, "Sir, step outside with me—"

Mason shook him off. He stumbled toward the door, grabbed Hugo by the arm, and pushed out into the night. Cole was trembling, leaning heavily against me. Deputy Bobby looked at us. A flash fire ran through me, and I couldn't meet his eyes.

Before Deputy Bobby could speak, Cole mumbled, "I'm going." He turned toward me, not quite looking at me, and mumbled, "I'm sorry." Then limped out of the bar.

The music was still playing, and I wanted to know how long this song could be, because it felt like it had been going for hours. Everyone was staring. Sweat prickled under my arms and across my back. I could feel myself shrinking inside my skin. Voices began to pick up—first whispers, then a laugh. I took another of those panicked looks, but the only door seemed to be the one that led out to the parking lot. I couldn't go that way; Mason and Cole and Hugo might be out there—any of them or all of them.

"Are you okay—" Deputy Bobby asked.

I managed to nod before I ran into the restroom and locked the door behind me.

Not to put too fine a point on it, but it wasn't exactly the ideal place to hide until civilization collapsed and we all reverted to roving bands of murderous scrappers. That was my initial plan. The restroom had a little hopper window that was open, and I stood under it where the air was cool and smelled like pine duff and wet concrete. After a while, when it became obvious that a *Mad Max-*

style apocalypse wasn't going to happen in the next five or ten minutes, I washed my face and dried off with paper towels.

I considered myself in the starting-to-tarnish mirror. Why did it have to be here? Why did it have to be tonight? Why did there have to be so many other people? Why did Deputy Bobby have to be one of them? And why couldn't I be a normal person and not freak out at the slightest social discomfort?

Mirror-me didn't have any answers. He also, because of the tarnish, occasionally looked like he didn't have any eyebrows. I made sure they were still there. I checked my phone for news of a nuclear missile strike headed to Hastings Rock. (Nothing.) Finally, I made myself unbolt the door. A guy with a flattop and a golf polo pushed past me with a desperation I knew all too well.

When I stepped out into the bar, nobody booed, hissed, or, uh, catcalled, I guess? A couple of people glanced at me. A woman I recognized from the general store gave me a commiserating smile. An older guy with tremendous nose hair offered a thumbs up. I smiled back—or, at least, I tried to until I heard Deputy Bobby's voice.

"I said I'm sorry. And I am sorry. But it's my job—"

"No, it's not." That was West. "You're not on duty. This was my night with Bobby, not with Deputy Mai. I want a night. I don't think that's too much to ask, do you?"

Deputy Bobby's silence lasted a beat longer than I expected, but his voice had its usual firm calm as he said, "No, it's not. But it's also not that simple—"

"Of course not." West sounded like he was crying. "I can't do this with you tonight. Not again." I thought maybe that was the end, but then West spoke again, his voice quavering with tears. "Don't you see? This is why we have to get out of this stupid town."

Movement on the other side of one of the pony walls drew my attention, and I caught a glimpse of West darting toward the door, wiping his eyes as he crossed the room.

I gave him a ten count, and then I left too. I told myself not to look back, but, of course, I did. Deputy Bobby was sitting alone in a booth, his head turned down over his beer, one hand buried in his thick, dark hair.

When I stepped outside, the night's cool damp felt like a balm against my fevered cheeks. A pair of headlights were swinging out onto the road, and I could make out the familiar silhouette of West's Jetta. The air smelled like cigarette smoke and weed and the lingering aroma of the Otter Slide's industrial fryer. Gravel crunched underfoot as I made my way toward the Jeep.

And then I saw the foot.

Somebody had too much to drink was my first thought. I stared at the sneaker sticking out from around the side of the Otter Slide. But it was a familiar sneaker. I knew that sneaker because I had, after eight agonizing weeks of indecision, bought that sneaker. For Hugo. For his birthday. And it had felt like a victory because he'd said he loved them. It always made me happy when I saw him wearing them. And I realized I hadn't even noticed that he'd been wearing them today, and I didn't know what to make of that.

I walked around the side of the building. Hugo lay in the deeper shadows there; it was easy to believe that nobody had seen him, not unless they caught a chance glimpse of his foot sticking out. I recognized his soft snore. Mason had left him here, like this. Not just passed out, but passed out in public, next to a parking lot, in a town where Hugo didn't know anyone. Mason hadn't cared, though; he'd been too angry after his fights with Penny and Cole. Or maybe Mason hadn't even noticed; Hugo had been blacking out, and Mason hadn't been far behind.

Crouching, I said, "Hugo, wake up. We've got to go."

Nothing came back to me except that soft snore.

I reached down to shake him. In all the years we'd been together, I'd never seen him trashed like this, and a part of me wondered if it was more than alcohol—if Mason, like his brother, indulged in other substances, and if he'd given Hugo something, maybe without Hugo even knowing. But as I was about to grab Hugo's shoulder, I stopped.

Something small and brown lay on his leg.

I leaned down to inspect it. It was a coconut bead, like the ones on Mason's necklace. I leaned back, trying to get more light, and spotted another bead. And another. They were all over the place like the necklace had snapped and the beads had flown everywhere. I started to breathe more quickly. My hands felt numb, and it was unexpectedly difficult to fumble my phone out of my pocket and turn on the flashlight.

He was lying a few feet away at the base of the dumpster. A wet smear, reddish black in the weak light, glistened on the side of the dumpster, marking where his head had slid along the metal. His eyes were half-closed and blank, and he wasn't breathing, and although I wasn't an expert, I knew as soon as I saw him that Mason was dead.

CHAPTER 5

I called 911. Then I went inside and got Deputy Bobby. He must have seen something on my face because, even though I could tell he was still upset, his expression immediately changed to detached professionalism. I took him to Hugo and Mason, and he checked both of them. Hugo, he pronounced okay. But I'd been right about Mason.

After I'd told Deputy Bobby everything, he put me in the Jeep and told me to get the heater going. When I couldn't get the keys in the ignition, he took them and did it for me.

He went back inside, and he must have said something to Seely, because nobody left the bar until the deputies arrived and set up a privacy barrier around Hugo and Mason. An ambulance came, and I couldn't see what they did behind the barrier, but I saw when the paramedics wheeled Hugo away on a stretcher. A van marked District Medical Examiner arrived, and more people went to work, setting up dozens of LED lights until the parking lot was bright enough to make my head throb.

Where was Cole? The question broke through the frozen numbness of my brain. I cupped my hands over the vents; I was still trembling, and even though it wasn't a cold night—cool, yes, but not cold—the heat felt good. And then a second question came: where was Penny?

A deputy named Winegar, heavyset and pouchy eyed, took my statement, and at Deputy Bobby's request, he said I could go home.

"Come on," Deputy Bobby said, a hand on my elbow as he urged me out of the Jeep.

"But he said I could go home."

"You're not driving."

Once I was settled in the Jeep's passenger seat, Deputy Bobby took the wheel. We eased out of the lot and headed south toward Hemlock House. We left Hastings Rock behind and entered the forest: lots of massive Sitka spruce, but fir and alder and pine too. Ferns so big and ancient-looking they would have made a dinosaur happy. The fog belt was thick tonight, and when we passed through it, it was like the only thing that existed was the inside of the Jeep, and me, and Deputy Bobby.

"How are you doing?"

"Fine."

"It's all right if you're not. That would have been a shock to anyone."

"Then I'm terrible."

Deputy Bobby's big, goofy grin flashed and then was gone. "Your friend is going to be fine."

I didn't know what to say to that, so I said, "I hope so."

He looked like he wanted to say more, but then we cleared the fog. The headlights cut little circles out of the night: the gray green of the trees and bracken, the blacktop, the reflectors winking back at us. We kept driving, and Deputy Bobby didn't say anything else.

When he pulled into the coach house, my brain finally cleared enough to ask, "Are you okay?"

"Of course."

"I don't mean, um, Mason."

He cocked his head.

"I know you're a big, burly police type."

He turned in his seat. He had a perfect, razor-sharp part in his hair. A perfect, razor-sharp jawline. Have I mentioned he had a perfect face?

"Nothing fazes you," I said. "You're the Man of Steel. You eat bad guys for breakfast. Actually, that seems super unhealthy, and definitely not Deputy Bobby approved. I bet you eat a grapefruit every morning. Zero bad guys."

"Dash."

"Maybe soaked oats?"

He gave me a look.

"With currants?"

"You're making me reconsider the definition of okay. What's going on?"

"I heard you and West." The words escaped me in a rush. And then, as I shrank down in my seat and tried not to die, "After Mason and Cole argued. I wasn't trying to eavesdrop, it just happened. And you're, you know, my friend, and I could tell you were unhappy, and I wanted to make sure, um, you're okay. Or something."

Deputy Bobby was silent for about ten seconds. On the Dashiell Dawson Dane scale of Social Terror, it was a nine-point-seven.

"That was pretty terrible for you, huh?" Deputy Bobby asked.

For some reason, that eased some of the tension in my body. "Oh my God, you have no idea."

"I appreciate you asking, but I'm fine."

I nodded.

"West and I are fine," Deputy Bobby said.

I waited.

"He's understandably upset. And I'm upset because he's upset."

In the distance, the ocean sounded like a vast, unending murmur.

Deputy Bobby pushed a hand through his hair, making it not quite so perfect (don't worry, it still had a certain charm). And then he breathed out hard and long, and his voice was small as he said, "God, he is so mad at me, and I feel like nothing I do—" He stopped. A moment passed, and then another. He opened the door, and as he got out, he said, "I shouldn't have said that. I shouldn't be talking about this." And then he shut the door.

I got out of the Jeep and found him waiting on the drive. As the coach house's overhead door rattled down, I said, "You can talk about it, though. If you ever want to."

He didn't say anything.

"I'm an excellent listener."

Deputy Bobby shifted his weight. "Let's get you inside."

"And because I'm literally the most awkward person on the planet, you never have to worry about saying the wrong thing. Because you won't even have a chance. I'll say the wrong thing first."

That made the corner of his mouth tick up.

"And because I'm your friend."

"What is it going to take to end this conversation?"

"You tell me all your secrets and let me braid your hair."

A rare laugh burst out of him. "Inside, Mr. Dane. And get some rest."

"Aye-aye, Deputy Bobby."

At the front door, though, we both stopped again. The silence had a rushing quality that I thought might be the sound of the waves, but it felt like more than that. Like something building and building, rolling back and forth between us.

"Just," I said, "the offer stands, you know? Whenever. Whatever."

He looked at me with an unsettling intensity before, finally, saying, "You're a good friend."

"Uh, not that good, because I realized I don't know how you're going to get home. Wait, is this, like, a thing for us?"

Deputy Bobby offered that huge, goofy grin again as a pair of headlights turned onto the drive.

"If I had waited five more seconds," I said.

"So close."

"Goodnight, Deputy Bobby."

"Goodnight, Dash."

CHAPTER 6

I woke at the crack of dawn the next morning. Well, ten-thirty was the crack of dawn somewhere in the world. It certainly felt like the crack of dawn. No judgment—you try getting up early after finding a body and then having an incredibly confusing conversation with someone who is, objectively, the perfect man.

The perfect man for someone else. For his boyfriend. Whom he currently has.

Not currently. That makes it sound temporary.

You know what I mean.

Oh my God, I thought, staring up at the canopy. Then I got in the shower.

After, I put my phone on speaker and called Hugo. As the phone rang, I got dressed. When the call went to voicemail, I said, "It's Dash. Answer the phone, please."

I called him again. I picked out jeans and a tee that showed a rainbow-colored controller and the word GAYMER. When the call went to voicemail again, I said, "I'm going to keep calling until you answer."

But five calls later, Hugo still hadn't answered.

I found Indira and Keme in the kitchen. Although most of Hemlock House was a beautifully preserved specimen of another era, the kitchen had been modernized (probably because people didn't want to continue cooking over an open fire, among other reasons). Indira had her sleeves pushed back, and flour coated her hands and apron as she kneaded bread at the table. Keme, barefoot and in a hoodie and shorts, threw me a peace sign.

"What's up, my brother?" I asked.

Keme looked at Indira.

"I know," Indira said. "He does it on purpose."

"I do it because I'm hip with the youths," I said.

Keme made a rude gesture, and I swear to God, I think Indira smiled.

Before I could verify, though, Indira said, "There are waffles ready to pop in the toaster."

I made a sharp turn toward said toaster.

"A reasonable amount of butter and syrup, please," Indira said. "Keme thinks you're on the fast track for diabetes."

"You can't get diabetes from syrup," I said—although, to be fair, I had used a considerable amount of the jug over the last couple of months. "It's from a tree. It's basically a vegetable."

Indira sighed. Keme rubbed his eyes.

I called Hugo a few more times as I waited for the waffles to warm, but by the time I sat down at the table with a plate (and, in spite of Keme dramatically widening his eyes in disbelief, yes, it was a reasonable amount of syrup), Hugo still hadn't answered.

"Where would the police take someone if they were hurt?" I asked between bites.

"Is this about what happened last night?" Indira asked as she transferred the dough to an oiled bowl. "I wondered if you were there. Millie said she heard you found that poor young man."

"Wait, Millie already knows?" And if Millie knew, that meant everybody would know by the end of the day. I told Keme and Indira about finding Mason and Hugo the night before and repeated my question. "Hugo's not answering, and even though I'd love for him to jump on the next plane back home, I kind of feel like I should at least check on him."

Indira and Keme exchanged a look. "Dash, you found him with Mason. I don't think he's in the hospital."

"But he was unconscious, so where would he—" I looked from Indira to Keme, and it was Keme's pained expression that made me stop. "But that's ridiculous. Hugo wouldn't—I mean, he couldn't have. He didn't even know Mason." I tried to find words, but they weren't coming; I couldn't wrap my head around the idea that Hugo might have been involved in Mason's death, or that the police could believe he was a suspect.

"I'm sure everything's all right," Indira said, and then she dusted her hands as though that settled the matter, but the confidence didn't carry to her expression. Keme, if anything, looked even more serious.

"I'm going to call Deputy Bobby," I said.

Keme shook his head vigorously, but I was already placing the call.

He didn't answer until the fifth ring, and he sounded exhausted. "What's up?"

"Did you arrest Hugo?"

His silence was the answer.

"I can't believe you!"

"I didn't arrest him personally, you know. Sheriff Acosta is taking the lead on this. It was her call. And, in case it matters, I think it was the right one."

"Are you kidding me?"

"Dash—" Indira tried.

"Hugo is one of the kindest, most patient, most caring people on the planet. He'd never hurt anyone."

"There's a lot we still don't know about last night—" Deputy Bobby began.

"He didn't kill Mason."

"You need to take a breath."

"Take a breath? This is unbelievable. What kind of police work are you doing? Because it feels like the 'whoever's most convenient' methodology, just like a couple of months ago!"

"He has injuries consistent with an altercation—"

"Who? Mason? Of course he does! You saw Penny try to claw his eyes out, and then he and Cole brawled like a couple of drunken frat boys."

"I'm talking about Hugo." Strain made his voice sound like it was about to snap, and a distant part of me recognized that Deputy Bobby, exhausted after a long night and a fight with West and now my...attitude, to put it politely, was about to lose his temper. He never would have said even this much, I realized, if he hadn't already been at the brink. "I'm sorry," he added in a more controlled voice. "I have to go." But then he added, "Dash, please stay out of this. Acosta told us that we're supposed to arrest you on obstruction charges if you start poking around."

I managed a dull goodbye, but he'd already broken the connection.

Keme was looking at me with something approaching disgust. Indira had her head down and was taking way too long to cover the bowl of dough.

When I called Deputy Bobby again, he answered on the second ring. "I know you're upset, but can we talk about this later—"

"I'm sorry."

He didn't disconnect, at least.

"I'm sorry," I said again. "I shouldn't have raised my voice. Or said those things about your job. I'm frustrated, and it does, kind of, feel like a repeat. But it wasn't right of me to lump you in with everyone else. You were more than fair to me, when I was the one in trouble, and you're my friend, and I'm sorry for how I acted."

His silence dragged on.

"Also," I said, "I realize you asked if we could talk about this later, and I ignored that, so, uh, I'm sorry about that. Too. On top of the other sorry."

Keme rubbed his eyes some more.

"Deputy Bobby?"

His voice sounded strange. "Uh, yeah."

"Yeah?"

"It's okay. You didn't have to—I get it."

"Okay." I drew out the word.

His voice got even weirder. "Apology accepted."

"What's happening right now?"

"I can't talk, Dash." And then, in that same strange voice, "Thank you for the apology."

Then he disconnected.

"Does anyone understand guys?" I looked at Keme. "What about you? Shouldn't you have an expert opinion?"

He did a big production: waving his hands, shaking his head. Indira caught a little smile, and I was surprised, even though the call had been so weird, to find that I was smiling too.

"I guess I should call Lyda." Until a few months ago, if you'd asked me, I wouldn't have had any idea who to call if I needed legal representation—particularly, legal representation in a murder trial. But life in Hastings Rock had taught me all sorts of interesting things, and one of those was to call Lyda Hayashi, attorney-at-law, when things got hairy.

As I picked up my phone, Fox stepped into the kitchen. Lyda's secretary answered, and a few minutes later, I was explaining the situation to Lyda herself. Meanwhile, Indira told Fox about Hugo being arrested for Mason's murder.

When I disconnected, with a promise from Lyda that she'd look into Hugo's situation, Fox said, "We're solving another murder?"

"No," I said.

Fox's eyebrows went up.

I shook my head. "Absolutely not."

"But Bobby told you they had physical evidence suggesting that Hugo and Mason fought—"

"I have full confidence in the justice system."

"And they already arrested Hugo, which means they must be pretty sure he's the one who did it."

"Deputy Bobby literally told me to stay out of this."

"Deputy Bobby isn't looking at the big picture. Now that they've got a suspect in custody, you know that their efforts are primarily going to be directed to proving he did it—not to chasing down new leads." To Keme's questioning look, they added, "I got that from *Law & Order*."

A part of me knew that Fox was right. Sort of. I mean, yes, *Law & Order* was amazing, but it was still a TV show. Law enforcement officers were people too. They suffered from confirmation bias like everyone else. Once they thought they knew the answer, they'd automatically start looking for additional evidence to confirm what they already believed. And it was a question of resources and priorities. They didn't have the manpower to chase down every possible lead, especially if they already had a suspect in custody and solid physical evidence.

"Sheriff Acosta is good at her job—" I tried.

"Sheriff Acosta is new at her job," Fox countered. "She's overwhelmed. This is a high-profile case. There's going to be a tremendous amount of pressure on her to solve it quickly and cleanly. The Gauthier-Meadows family will want justice, and they'll want it fast, and they'll want it neat."

"Okay, but—"

"So, you need to step in."

"Why me?"

"Because you're so good at this," Fox said. "You're a natural. I mean, I'm good at it, too, but I can't because I have to spend the weekend sitting on my couch crying and watching *Below Deck*."

"Uh."

"Fox," Indira said, "tone it down a bit. Dash, Fox is right: you're good at this, and I'm not sure there's anyone else."

"But." I stopped there. I could think of all sorts of other people. Private investigators, for example. Lyda would probably know one. But how long would it take before they could start? And how much would they cost? I was tapped out until another wedding party decided to book Hemlock House (or until I sold the Great American Novel, and neither seemed likely in the immediate future). And Hugo, although he'd learned to dress the part, didn't come from money; he'd gotten a good advance on his first novel, but not enough to finance a legal defense, including a private investigator.

"Unless, of course," Fox said, examining their nails, "you hate Hugo, and you want to see him suffer in the most publicly humiliating way possible—"

"Okay!" I snapped. "You made your point."

Fox grinned. "We're going to solve a murder."

"We're going to find something to exonerate Hugo, and then we're going to leave the rest of it to the sheriff's office."

Keme had his arms folded across his chest, and he was staring at me, his expression dark.

"I know," I said to him. "I know it's risky. I know it's stupid."

He nodded slowly to let me know how stupid it was.

"But I don't know what else to do."

His expression hardened into a scowl. His eyes were fixed on mine, and his chest rose with quick, sharp breaths. Indira touched his shoulder, but he jerked away from her. Even that wasn't enough to break his gaze, though; I was the one who looked away first.

"Now," Fox said, "we should start with the most obvious suspect—"

My phone buzzed with an unknown number. I looked at the others. Fox shrugged. Keme shook his head. Indira said, "Maybe it's Hugo."

I had a mental image of Hugo standing at a payphone in a cellblock, and even though my brain informed me that the Ridge County jail probably didn't have cellblocks, it was still enough to make me accept the call.

But instead of Hugo's voice, it was Cole.

"Uh, hi, Cole," I managed to say. And then, because it was the only thing I could think of, "I'm so sorry about Mason."

Keme gestured frantically to the phone. Indira whispered, "Put it on speaker."

I did, and Cole's voice floated out into the room, sounding flat, almost affectless as he said, "Thanks."

"How are you doing?"

"Not great." He tore off a little laugh. Fox's eyebrows went up. "Really not great, actually. How are you?" Before I had to answer, he said, "I wanted to apologize about last night."

"What?"

"About all of it. About how I acted. That stupid fight." His voice hitched. "About showing up high. And then going to the bathroom to get high. God, I'm high right now. What is wrong with me?"

Keme rolled his eyes.

Cole continued, "I, uh, wanted to say that you're a great guy, and I should have listened when you told me, you know, what you wanted me to do. Or not do. And I'm sorry. You deserve better than that."

"You don't have to apologize. I'm so sorry for what you're going through." And then, because it was automatic, I heard myself say, "If you need anything—"

"Yes, God, please." Another of those jagged laughs came across the line. "I have to get out of this house. I'm going crazy."

My silence must have carried my shock.

"Not, like, a date," Cole mumbled. "I need to talk to someone, and you were so sweet, and I know you're going to think I'm just saying this, but I feel like we connected." He stopped, and I thought I could hear him swallow through tears as he fought for a self-mocking tone. "And you know what is so freaking pathetic? I don't have anybody else. Who am I going to call? Some college kid who sells me E?"

I still had no idea what to say.

"Never mind," Cole said. "This was stupid. I'm sorry I bothered you."

Fox grabbed my elbow. They gave me a shake and pointed at the phone, and I said, "What?"

"Huh?" Cole said.

"Uh, a second." I put the phone on mute and said again to Fox, "What?"

"Tell him yes," Fox said.

"Are you out of your mind? He's a thirty-year-old man-child. I mean, yes, he's sweet, and yes, I feel bad for him, and yes, he does have that whole I'm-so-handsome-I-could-be-a-watch-model thing going for him—"

"What is wrong with you?"

"I'm anxious, I'm a perfectionist, I've got crippling self-doubt, I'm bad at relationships—"

Keme was giving Indira a significant look and tapping his wrist, probably because I'd let that watch-model comment slip.

Indira said, "Don't tease him."

"I know all that," Fox said, waving away my words. "I'm talking about this, right now. Hugo is in prison—"

"He's in jail, technically."

Very slowly, Fox said again, "What is wrong with you?"

I decided not to answer that.

"Cole got into a huge fight with Mason last night," Fox said. "Remember? And not long after, Mason was dead."

"Yeah, but—" I stopped and gestured at the phone. "Listen to him. He's a wreck."

"Or he's an excellent actor. Either way, this is an ideal opportunity."

"For what? To go on a date with a bereaved potential murderer?"

Keme blew out a long breath.

"I know, dear," Indira said. "They're both dramatic." To me, she said, "Dashiell, say yes. His grief could be real, and he could still be the killer;

emotions run high in that family, and it wouldn't be the first time someone did something terrible and then regretted it."

"I can't believe you're encouraging this."

"What about you?" I asked Keme.

He leaned across the table to smack me—not so lightly—upside the head.

"How is that supposed to be helpful?"

Keme cocked a grin, and Fox said, "I think that was more for his own benefit."

"I have crazy people for friends," I said as I reached for my phone. "This is why I end up in these shenanigans."

"Some people would consider themselves fortunate—" Fox began, but they cut off when I glared at them.

After unmuting the phone, I said, "Cole?"

"Hey, I'm going to get out of here for a little while. Go for a run. I'm sorry I bothered you."

"You didn't bother me. I know what it's like to be lonely and not have anyone to talk to. I'm a little busy right now, but could we get together this evening?"

The relief was transparent in his voice. "Yes, God, thank you."

After agreeing to figure out a location over text, we disconnected.

"Now if you could only apply these sleuthing skills," Fox said, "to find yourself a man who isn't a potential killer."

"Why are you here?" I asked.

"Because I didn't know what to do with all the centerpieces I made for the wedding. I thought maybe you still wanted them."

"Why would I—" I got to my feet so quickly the chair scraped across the floor. "Actually, yes, that's perfect. Come with me."

"Where are you going?" Indira asked.

"To figure out who might have wanted to kill Mason."

CHAPTER 7

"I'm asking if you're sure," Fox said. We were in their van—an ancient Toyota that made ominous creaking noises every time we drove over an uneven patch of road—driving toward the Gauthier-Meadowses' beach house. The van was full of cardboard boxes, tissue paper, plastic tubs of shells and sea glass, an enormous silk sunflower, and so many bolts of tulle that it looked like a bride (or maybe several brides) had exploded. It also smelled strongly of...something. The air freshener hanging from the rearview mirror said DRAGON MUSK. "We could wait for them to leave."

"That might be too late," I said. We went over a steel plate, and I swear to God, the van shivered. "Someone killed Mason, and we need to figure out who—and why. And the best way to do that is to begin our victimology."

"That does sound better than saying 'snoop around in a house full of people.'"

I chose to ignore that, but when the van gave another shudder, I had to say, "Fox, how old is this thing?"

"Instead of giving the sheriff a wonderful reason to arrest you, why don't you talk to Penny? I mean, she attacked him. Shouldn't that make her the number one suspect?"

"It's got a cassette player." I pushed the eject button. "It's got an original Olivia Newton-John *Totally Hot* cassette in the cassette player."

"Don't touch that," Fox said. "If this were an episode of *Law & Order*—"

"I know: Penny attacked him. And I'm sure the sheriff has talked to her. But we need to learn whatever we can about Mason. And, side note, Penny was the maid of honor. No matter how angry she was, Sharian has to be angrier. I mean, she's the jilted bride. Think about it: in the space of a few hours, Sharian went from thinking she was going to marry a rich man, to learning that he planned to give all his money away, to discovering that—when push came to shove—he'd rather call off the wedding than keep the money, to having her ex-fiancé go hook up with a random guy."

"But Sharian wasn't at the bar."

"She didn't come inside the bar," I said. "Maybe she'd been following him. Maybe she saw him with Hugo and decided to go after him, and then she sat in the parking lot, working herself up until he came outside."

"That's a lot of maybes."

Ahead of us, an unmarked drive led up a wooded hill. A deputy's cruiser was pulled across the entrance, and a stoop-shouldered older man in uniform was reading what appeared to be a copy of *TV Guide.*

"Remember," I said as I squirmed between the seats and under a cloud of tulle. "Keep it simple."

"Don't teach your grandmother to suck eggs."

"What?"

Instead of answering, Fox hissed and waved for me to get down, and a moment later, I heard the window groan as Fox lowered it. I did a final wiggle to get as deeply under the tulle as I could, and then I heard a man say, "What've we got here?"

For a single, panicked moment, I thought he'd spotted me—I had that unshakeable feeling that some part of me was sticking out somewhere, perfectly visible.

But Fox's reply was unruffled. "Hello, Bruce."

"Can't go in there."

"Sorry, but I have to. I've got all these centerpieces for the wedding, and they're due today."

"There's not going to be a wedding. You can turn around and head home."

"What do you mean there's no wedding? I made a hundred and seventy-five centerpieces. There's going to be a wedding if I have to drag you to the altar and get hitched myself."

That, I thought, definitely didn't fall under the heading of keep it simple.

"The groom's dead. Somebody broke his head open—killed him right outside the Otter Slide. Bashed him good on the dumpster. Brains everywhere."

And that, I thought, fell under the heading of majorly fibbing.

"Blood?" Fox asked.

"Gallons of it. Course, it didn't bother me. A man's got to do what a man's got to do. In this job, you see things like that, you do."

"Give me a break," I said under my breath.

"What was that?" the deputy asked.

"I said give me a break," Fox said a little too loudly. "I mean, you've got to let me up there, Bruce. Even if the wedding is off, they've still got to pay me, right? And they're not going to do that unless I show up and deliver the centerpieces."

"Well," the deputy said. And then he whistled. "I don't know."

"Move your car, you old goose," Fox said, "and I'll buy you a drink sometime."

"I shouldn't. But I'm gonna hold you to that drink."

A moment later, an engine grumbled to life, and then the van started forward again.

"Ta," Fox called through the window, and the deputy called a goodbye after us. We started up the hill, and the van turned twice before Fox said, "You can come out now."

I emerged from under the sea of tulle, wiping my face. "How in the world can it be so hot down there?"

"Imagine being a bride."

"Did you flirt with a man who tried to brag about gallons of blood?"

"Yes," Fox said, "and you're welcome."

"Uh, thank you." And then, because I couldn't resist: "So, like, are you two..."

In answer to the trailing-off question, Fox said primly, "Don't be ridiculous."

I tried to let it go. But somehow, I got a picture of Bruce and Fox, hot and heavy in the back of the van, with DRAGON MUSK air freshener and Olivia Newton-John to set the mood. Will Gower (the fictional detective who lived in my head) would have taken that as his cue to drink himself into oblivion. All I could do was try to think about baseball—that was what straight guys did, I was told—but since I didn't know anything about baseball, I thought about Dungeons and Dragons. I tried to remember all the stats for a mind flayer. Yes, as a matter of fact, I am that nerdy.

Fortunately, we crested the hill and came to the Gauthier-Meadowses' home. Vacation home, I guess. It was perched on the back of the hill, with a breathtaking view of forested slopes stretching down to the sun-stitched waters of the Pacific. The house itself belonged to the coastal modern style: a swooping semicircle of concrete and glass. Windows opened every wall, and the effect was one of a fishbowl. Or a hothouse. Two identical dark Mercedes sedans were parked in the circular drive.

"Are you sure this is a good idea?" Fox asked.

"Well," I said.

"Oh my God. Forget I asked."

"Just help me get inside."

Fox made a face, but they slid out of their seat and headed toward the front door. I grabbed my burgling gear (a pair of disposable gloves from home) and tried not to have a heart attack. Or a panic attack. Really, zero attacks of any kind was the idea.

The front door opened, and Penny the ex-maid-of-honor stepped out. She was wearing a hoodie monogrammed with a P (the top of the letter was shaped like a heart), and she had her long hair pulled over one shoulder, and the makeup was in full force. Fox said something, and Penny glanced at the van. Then she said something and went back inside. A moment later, the garage door began to rattle up.

When Fox returned to the van, they said, "That poor girl had no idea what to say. She told us to put everything in the garage for now."

Fox and I each grabbed a box, and we carried them into the garage. No cars, I noticed—I guessed everybody had parked outside while the weather was clear. I deposited my box next to Fox's along one wall. There were no tools hanging on the wall. There was no junk stashed in the corners. The concrete slab didn't even have any oil stains. I knew this was a vacation home, and so maybe it didn't get used much, but it still gave the place an empty, unreal quality, the way rental properties sometimes had.

"Hurry," Fox said. "I'll drag this out as long as I can."

"Thank you for doing this."

Fox waved me toward the house. I tried the door that led in from the garage, and it opened. On the other side was a laundry room. A few cleaning supplies sat on a shelf above a high-end washer and dryer, and the air smelled like Tide. Grains of sand speckled the floor. Another door stood open, connecting with what appeared to be a mudroom—slickers and jackets hung from hooks on the wall, with sneakers and flip-flops on trays on the floor. Built-in cabinets suggested storage for more outdoor gear.

I stopped at the next door, which was closed, and listened. I thought maybe I could hear a TV in the distance, but it was hard to tell if that was real or my imagination. My heart was beating faster, and I clutched the disposable gloves in one sweaty hand. I'd put those on later—if I wore them now and someone caught me, it would be a lot harder to explain that I'd knocked and I was sorry and I desperately needed to use the bathroom.

After a five-count, I opened the door and stepped into a short hallway. To my right, it doglegged toward what I thought must be a bedroom. To my left, I glimpsed a kitchen and then a living area. I wasn't sure what I was looking for other than, well, anything that might help me understand who had killed Mason and why. My primary target would be Mason's bedroom; victimology was a key part of any homicide investigation, as Detective Will Gower of the, uh, LAPD (maybe?) would tell you. Of course, I had to *find* his room first.

I turned right and started down the dogleg hall. Then something crunched underfoot.

I froze. The crunching sound had seemed enormous, and I waited for the inevitable shouts of alarm. But seconds passed, and then a minute, and the shouts never came. I eased my weight back and saw that I'd stepped on gravel someone had tracked in from the driveway. As I was about to pick a path around the loose stones, a voice floated out to me through a doorway down the hall.

It took me a moment to recognize Gary's voice. Mason's father sounded more annoyed than grief stricken as he said, "Yes, I need to change an order. The last name is Meadows. Yes, what did she tell you? Right. Right. Okay, well, I think there was a miscommunication. Could you change the delivery time for half an hour later? Perfect. Thanks." Silence came, and then the sound of an e-cig. When he spoke again, it sounded like he was talking to himself, and his voice held an adolescent's impotent rage. "Tell me what to do, you cow."

I headed back the way I'd come as quietly as I could. When I reached the opening to the kitchen, I listened again. I still didn't hear anything. I risked a look. It was a long, open space that flowed into what was probably called the great room. The countertops looked like marble. The cabinets were clearly custom. Lots of brushed nickel and white tile and vivid pops of blue. One wall was clad in a driftwood veneer that had, undoubtedly, cost a fortune.

The coast was clear, so I hurried down the length of the kitchen. Ahead of me, French doors led out onto a lanai, and beyond that, I could make out a pool.

(Of course they had a pool.) A hallway cut off to the right, and an open door revealed a powder room.

From the other side of the great room came the sound of a door opening, and then a woman saying, "Because it's my money." The voice belonged to Jodi, the grandmother. "And I'll do whatever I want with it."

Another woman—Becky—responded. "Of course you will." Mason's mom sounded like a woman holding on to the last threads of her temper. "When have you not?"

The voices were coming towards me, so I darted into the powder room and nudged the door shut.

"Who's worked day and night for you?" Becky asked. "Who's earned that money? Who, Mother?"

"I've made my decision," Jodi said. "It's final."

The voices were still coming toward me. I glanced around the darkened powder room. Behind me, a second door had a strip of light under it. I crept over to it and tried the handle, and it opened silently. On the other side was the lanai, with its wicker furniture and brightly colored pillows and potted plants.

"You're acting like a petulant child," Becky said. "Mason hasn't even been dead a day. Show a modicum of respect."

The unmistakable sound of a slap rang out, and Becky let out a wordless cry that sounded like it came from the kitchen. I slipped out onto the lanai and shut the door behind me.

Adrenaline hammered through me. My head was swimmy. My skin felt greasy. I couldn't seem to get enough air. This was, a far-off, clinical part of me noted, a terrible idea, and I made a solemn vow never, ever, ever again to write a sneaking-around scene for Will Gower, private investigator. Not ever. And then, because my other option was to throw up out of sheer nerves, I started moving again.

To my right, another pair of French doors connected with what had to be a bedroom jutting off from the main building. These doors had curtains drawn, but imperfectly—a gap remained where they didn't quite meet, and movement on the other side caught my eye. There was something about the movement, something about how hurried it appeared, a hint of furtiveness, that reminded me of, well, me. So, I moved closer, because I wanted to know who else was sneaking around inside the Gauthier-Meadowses' vacation home.

When I peered through the opening in the curtains, I saw a bedroom. The usual bedroom furniture. An oil painting of the sea cliffs. Clothing—a man's and a woman's—piled on the floor. And that meant this had to be Mason and Sharian's room—the only other couple was Gary and Becky, and I'd already found their room. As I watched, Penny stepped out of the en suite bathroom. She was rummaging through what appeared to be, of all things, a dopp kit. Her face was snarled with frustration, and she pawed at the contents of the dopp kit with what looked like despair.

"Penny?"

The voice was so close and so loud that I startled and almost bumped the glass. I braced myself with one hand on the wall and tried to swallow my heart. On the other side of the French doors, Penny was frantically returning the dopp kit to the bathroom. A moment later, she called, "Do you need something?" and slipped out of the bedroom.

Why, I wanted to know, was Penny creeping around in Mason and Sharian's room? And what had she been looking for?

I tried the handle on the French door, and it opened. Apparently, when you were as wealthy as the Gauthier-Meadows clan, you never had to lock anything. Or maybe they trusted that the lanai would be secure, and they didn't need to bother with the doors that led into the house proper. Or maybe Mason had been more like Cole than it seemed—a man-child who'd never had to take care of himself.

Whatever the reason, it was my good luck. I moved into the bedroom and pulled on my gloves.

I started in the bathroom and found the dopp kit that Penny had been searching. It was olive-colored canvas, and it held men's deodorant (an all-natural brand that I'd never heard of), a toothbrush that looked like it was based on alien technology, floss (Oral-B), a lotion for men with sensitive skin (why it was specifically for men was unclear to me—presumably, some women also had sensitive skin), and a tin of hair wax that I'd once considered buying Hugo for his birthday. In the end, I hadn't bought it for him because a) I'm the master of indecision, and b) it cost approximately the same, ounce per ounce, as gold.

I didn't see any pills. I didn't find cash hidden inside a trick can of shaving cream (yes, that featured in one of the Will Gower sleuthing episodes, and I'm not accepting feedback at this time). I didn't see anything, in other words, that would explain what Penny had been looking for, or why she'd been snooping in here.

Finally, I had to give up, and I returned the dopp kit to the counter. Sharian had a toiletry bag here as well, and I checked that, but aside from her penchant for outrageously expensive cosmetics, I didn't discover anything there either. I checked the time on my phone. Unbelievably, I'd been inside the Gauthier-Meadowses' home for less than five minutes. It felt longer. It felt like I was that guy at the end of *Indiana Jones and the Last Crusade*, and I was nothing but desiccated flesh over ancient bones and surprisingly beautiful hair (for a corpse). I figured Fox could stall for another five minutes. Maybe, at the outside, ten.

I started my search. It might seem like being a writer (I was, technically, a writer, even if I hadn't written anything this week—okay, this month) wouldn't lend itself to, well, skullduggery and general poking and prowling and ferreting about. But I wasn't an ordinary writer. I was a mystery writer. (Okay, if I was being honest, it had been at least six weeks.) And I'd grown up with parents who were mystery writers. And everything we'd talked about, day and night and at meals and before bed, had been about hot shots and throwaway pieces and how to murder somebody by causing an embolism. Mystery writers learned all sorts of weird stuff that wasn't great conversation material at most parties but could be, under the right conditions, surprisingly useful. For example, in one story, Will Gower, amateur sleuth, had learned all about secret hiding places because he ran a death cleaning company. He was always turning up valuable clues that the police had missed because he was such a thorough cleaner. (As you might imagine, this story is still in a preliminary draft form.) But because of that story, I'd done a lot of research about hiding places inside homes.

Not that it was any help. Because I didn't find anything.

As far as I could tell, there wasn't anything to find. I started with their luggage, and I found nothing but clothes and shoes. I tried the dresser. More clothes. Mason's wallet was gone. Sharian's purse held the usual assortment of tissues and lip gloss and a wallet with no cash but enough credit cards to play blackjack. I did a Will Gower-style search (I had an idea for a story where he was a dorm RA, and he had to do cleaning checks). There was nothing hidden inside the toilet tank, or in the hollow-core door, or behind a baseboard. I didn't find any drugs. I didn't find any incriminating photos. I didn't find any blackmail demands. I found nothing. Not a single thing to help me understand who might have killed Mason. I definitely didn't find anything to clear Hugo's name.

My time was almost up. I put everything back as best I could, stripped off the gloves, and—after checking that it was clear—let myself out onto the lanai. Since my time for searching was up, I decided the best thing to do would be to exit through the back and go around the side of the house. Less chance that way of being, you know, spotted and arrested.

As I crossed the patio and made my way around the pool, I fought a wave of disappointment. Apparently, being a mystery writer didn't actually prepare you for saving your ex-boyfriend from a murder charge. I'd been sure that I would learn something about Mason that would put me on the right track, and instead, I'd taken a huge risk for no reason—I'd hit a dead end.

I was still feeling sorry for myself as I came around the corner of the house and crashed into someone. We both stumbled back. It took me a moment to reorient myself. I stared in shock at Sharian, and the ex-bride-to-be stared back at me. And then, her voice rising in outrage, she said, "Hey, what are you doing back here?"

CHAPTER 8

For a moment, I couldn't believe my bad luck: I'd made it through that whole stupid house without getting caught, and on my way out—when I was taking the safe route, thank you much—it had all fallen apart.

Then I realized maybe this was my chance.

Sharian was right here in front of me. The ex-bride-to-be.

And statistically, the victim's partner was the most likely culprit.

"Looking for you." The words popped out of my mouth before I could consider them. I rubbed my head and gave an attempt at a wry grin. "Sorry about that."

Sharian huffed an annoyed breath, but she did look slightly…gratified, maybe?

"I'm sick," she said, as though that explained something. But she didn't look sick. She looked sun-kissed and blond and perfectly tousled, and keeping it all up was probably the equivalent of a three-ring circus. Maybe she was trying to draw attention away from the phone she was clutching in one hand because she brought the other to her head and said, "I have the worst migraine."

"I'm so sorry."

"And my vertigo."

"Uh, do you need to sit down?"

She did a delicate little cry—real tears, ladies and gentlemen. She was still trying to hide the phone by keeping it low and tight to her side. "I miss him so much."

Which might actually have been true; death had a way of sharpening some edges and blunting others, and although Sharian might have been angry with Mason (or, more specifically, angry about his plan to get rid of his money), people were complicated. Her anger at Mason might have coexisted with the love and affection that had brought them together, and maybe death had made it easier to set aside her resentment.

I mean, technically anything was possible.

"Oh my God," she said, "I think I'm going to pass out."

I helped her back to the patio and onto one of the chaises. Then I pulled over a chair for myself and sat. It was one of those late summer days on the coast that was perfect: not a trace of a cloud in the sky, warm enough for a T-shirt and shorts while you were sitting in the sun, but you'd want a jacket in a breeze or the shade. Below us, the slopes of fir and cedar glistened blue-green in the light, and beyond the trees, the waves came in like ruffled lace.

Sharian did not pass out, by the way.

I sat with her, breathing in the smell of the pool—chlorine and water on ceramic tile—and the resinous sweetness of the trees and something faint and floral, probably her perfume. I waited.

My phone vibrated with a text from Fox: *Where are you?*

I texted back: *Almost done.*

After another minute, Sharian opened her eyes.

"Any better?" I asked.

She made a faint noise of complaint and, in a weak voice, asked, "You said you were looking for me?"

"Uh, yes. To offer my condolences." And then, before I knew what I was doing, I said, "I know what it's like, a little. When your relationship falls apart, and your life goes with it."

She looked at me. The water lapped restlessly in the pool.

"I'm sorry," I said. "I shouldn't be bothering you."

"Everyone thinks I was mad about the money," she said. The words were clear, detached. They had nothing of the delicate daisy with a terrible migraine. "Or about the cheating. Or about the fact that every time he turned around, he had cold feet. They're all talking about it. Even though the sheriff arrested that man, they're all talking about me, like I did this. They're all so awful. Can you blame Mason for wanting to get away from them?"

"I didn't realize Mason wasn't close with his family."

"How could he be close with—with that? A dragon, an ice queen, and that little weasel. You've seen them. Jodi wants them all to be her little puppets. Becky's practically a robot; all she does is work. And when Gary isn't being emasculated in public by Becky, he's coming up with pathetic little power plays to drive her crazy."

"I thought I heard him on the phone earlier," I confessed. "It sounded like he was changing an appointment or a delivery or something."

"Oh sure. Anything to mess with Becky's head. You should see them. She says stop, he says go. She says hot, he says cold. It could be anything—God, they argue about takeout versus delivery." She smoothed a hand down her shirt. "Cole's the only one that's a human being, and he's even more messed up than Mason. God, I cannot believe I dragged Penny into this mess."

"I guess the deputies have been pretty hard on you."

"Not really. They were nice, actually. When the sheriff came this morning to…to tell us, she was nice. I didn't know there were lady sheriffs."

"Huh," I said. And then I fibbed. "I heard them talking about where you were last night."

"Where I was? I was here. Where else was I going to be? I don't have a car. I don't have any friends. We were stuck here, especially once Mason decided to abandon me." She must have forgotten about trying to hide her phone from me, because now she toyed with it in her lap. "And he called me selfish—can you believe that? I have a right to expect financial security, don't I? I have a right to expect my partner to take care of me. I don't think that's too much to ask. I put up with all his whining and moaning, all the nights he'd lie there on the floor telling me how hard his life was because he had so much money and how guilty he felt, on and on. I put up with a lot, I think. I put in my time. And then he was going to give it all away without even telling me? Well, it was my money too. That's what I think. We were going to get married, and that meant it was my money too!"

Her anger left her flushed by the time she finished. She sat, breathing hard, staring out at the ocean. I hadn't noticed until now, but she was wearing her engagement ring—a massive rock that caught the light and splintered it into a rainbow shimmer across her leg. Still, I wondered. Or again?

"What was that all about?" I asked. "Giving away the money?"

Sharian snorted. "Don't get me started. The whole family is weird about money. Grandma Jodi uses it to control Becky. Becky uses it to control Gary. Gary's so desperate for it that he sticks around no matter how badly Becky treats him; I think he's hoping that when Jodi dies, she'll leave him something of his own, which goes to show how stupid he is. Mason spent his whole life feeling he'd done something wrong somehow, like he ought to feel bad because he had a trust fund waiting for him." In a rush, she added, "Don't get me wrong: I loved Mason. And I was so proud of him, all the good work he did. He was so generous and kind. But that's family money. And he had a family of his own to take care of. That should have been his responsibility, don't you think?"

"Does Cole feel guilty about the money too?"

"Cole's always too stoned to feel anything about anything. That's all he does: gets high so he doesn't have to deal with the fact that he's a waste of space." She turned the phone in her hands, her ring catching the light, and those prismatic glimmers streaked across the chaise. "He and Mason fought about everything. Put them in the same room, and they couldn't breathe the same air without getting into it. It's not their fault, I guess. Becky and Gary left them pretty messed up. Mason didn't talk about it a lot, but I picked up enough to get an idea. Becky was always at work. Gary was—well, God, you've met him. The boys had a nanny. Then they went to school. If they wanted something, Gary and Becky bought it for them, even if it wasn't for sale. One time, Mason told me they got one of his teachers fired because of something he'd said to Mason—he wouldn't say what, but I got the impression it was one of the reasons Mason always felt guilty about all that money. And he told me about another time, about how they'd bought Cole's way onto a baseball team in high school— even though Cole wasn't good enough. Those kids don't mess around, you know? They're serious about the game, and they made Cole's life miserable. He quit, and I think that was the last time he ever really tried at anything."

Water splashed against tile, and it sent pale, reflected light bobbing in the shadows of the lanai. I was thinking about my own parents, about all the award ceremonies and banquets and writing retreats, about the empty house and the empty hours. They'd never tried to buy my way onto a baseball team, but when I'd been ready to start sending out manuscripts, querying agents, they'd had Phil in their pocket, ready to go. I wasn't sure I could put into words why I'd said no, why I kept saying no. Even if I'd been able to tell her, I wasn't sure Sharian would understand. But Mason would have, I thought. And Cole definitely would.

"He promised he'd take me to try out for *The Voice*," Sharian said, and for the first time, her tears sounded genuine. She touched her eyes; she was still staring out at the restless Pacific. "God, I'm going to be so pitchy after all this crying."

"You said something about Mason having cold feet. Before you called off the wedding, I mean."

"Oh God. Every time, it was the exact same thing. That's why yesterday, as soon as the fight started, I knew what he was going to do. He gets on one of those stupid apps and finds somebody and thinks he's going to make me jealous." She let out a scoffing little laugh. "He's terrified of ending up like his parents. Loveless marriage. The fighting. All those issues about money—maybe that's why he thought he had to give it away."

"But wasn't it already an issue? The money, I mean."

"God, I wish. Cole and Mason don't get access to their trusts until they're thirty-one; that's what Grandma Jodi decided. It's family money, that's what she says. It's for the family. And that's what Mason and I talked about too—that money was for our family, and we needed to get married to start a family, and that kind of thing. Well, take somebody like Mason, who grew up with parents like that, is it a surprise he freaked out every time we talked about marriage? Every few months, it'd be the same conversation: are we in love? I don't know how I feel. Why am I so messed up? I wish I knew what it felt like to love someone."

For a moment, I couldn't say anything. All I could do was watch the reflected light from the pool rise and fall in the darkness of the lanai.

Sharian didn't seem to notice my silence. She shrugged. "He'd always come back and apologize, of course. He loved me—he did." A little too late, she corrected herself: "We were in love. But God, that boy had so many hangups, it was a full-time job keeping his head on straight. I guess that's over now."

"What are you and Penny going to do?"

"Jodi wants us to stay. Probably because I told her she's like my grandma too, even with Mason gone. That's what family does—stick together, you know." It sounded so scripted that I wondered how long it had taken her to come up with it. "I can't run off and leave them now."

"Sharian, I need to ask you something. You told me that everyone thinks you were upset about the money, and about the cheating, and about—well, everything Mason did. But I don't think that. I think you cared about Mason, even though he was confused and hurting and made a lot of mistakes."

Her eyes slid from the ocean to me. Her hands stilled in her lap.

"And I think you know, like I know, that what happened last night wasn't a terrible accident."

She said nothing, but I saw it in her face: confirmation. And fear.

"Do you know who might have wanted to hurt Mason?" I asked.

"The sheriff arrested somebody." Sharian's words were stiff, almost tongue tied. "She told Becky; I heard her."

"But it's the wrong person. I know it's the wrong person. And I think you know it too."

Her breathing hitched. The sun was high enough that now she looked washed out. Pale.

"Please," I said. "I know I'm asking a lot, but this is important. If you know anything that could help—"

When she spoke, her voice was rushed and breathy. "She said she was home all night. She said she was home with Gary and Becky all night, but I know she wasn't. I saw her leave."

"Who?" I asked. "Penny?"

"Jodi." Her voice was a breath now. "She was so angry. She said—she said she'd kill him. Those were her exact words. She said she'd kill him herself before she let him ruin the family like this."

Behind us, a door opened, and a voice said, "Mr. Dane, I'd like a word with you."

I turned in my seat. Sheriff Acosta stood in the doorway to the lanai.

Sheriff Acosta (technically, acting Sheriff Acosta) was a stocky woman in a khaki uniform. Her skin was a warm brown, her eyes were tawny, and she had her dark hair pulled back into a ponytail. She gelled her baby hairs to her forehead, and they almost hid the faint scar on her temple. Right then, her face was set and neutral, even though she still managed to radiate disapproval.

"Right now," she added.

"Please don't say anything," Sharian whispered.

I nodded, mostly because I didn't know what to say or whom to say it to, and rose and followed the sheriff.

She led me through the house, past the icy stares of Jodi, Becky, and Gary. No sign of Penny—maybe she was back in Mason's room, oh-so-suspiciously searching for something. When we stepped outside, the sheriff pulled the front door shut. Then she gave me a long look.

One of those things you learn as a mystery writer? Law enforcement types love to use silence as a weapon. Special Agent Will Gower of the FBI was known for his stony silences that caused even the most hardened criminal to break down and confess.

It is a good tool, though, and finally I said, "Fox is waiting—"

"Mr. Dane, I want to get a few things clear. I understand that my predecessor caused you a lot of problems. And I also understand that you played an important role in resolving matters."

That was an understated way of saying that the previous sheriff had helped Vivienne Carver fake her own death and let me take the fall for it, and the only reason I was still a free man was that I had found Vivienne and tricked a confession out of her (admittedly, with the help of my friends).

"I also understand that you're smart and you're curious and you are—" Her mouth soured around the word. "—knowledgeable, to a degree, about criminal justice."

I wondered who had told her I was smart and curious. Deputy Bobby, maybe? I wanted to know if he'd talked about me. If he'd talked to her about me, I mean. That was a strange, fluttering thought, that maybe sometimes Deputy Bobby said something about me in passing—*Last weekend? Oh, Dash and I went on a hike.* Or *No big plans for my day off; I'll probably swing by Hemlock House to see Dash.*

"But," Acosta said, drawing me back to the present, "you are also a civilian. You are not a peace officer. You are not a sheriff's deputy. You have no authority to investigate crimes."

"I know."

"Even though you feel like this case is personal. Even though you have a preexisting relationship with Mr. Fairchild."

"Hugo didn't do this."

"I'm taking the time to have this conversation with you as a courtesy—"

"Tell me why Hugo would have killed him. Give me one reason."

"—as a courtesy—"

"You can't. Hugo didn't have a reason to hurt Mason. There's no way he killed him."

"—because you're a citizen of Hastings Rock and because I understand that your relationship with the Sheriff's Office is complicated—"

"You're making a huge mistake."

"—and so, I wanted to be the one to talk to you about this and explain that, regardless of what happened in the past, I will not tolerate any interference in my investigations. Do I make myself clear?"

"You can't tell me why he'd do it. You can't even tell me how he'd do it. When I saw him, Hugo was so drunk he could barely stand. How could he have murdered Mason?"

"People who are intoxicated get in fights, Mr. Dane. They have poor judgment. Reduced impulse control. And manslaughter isn't the same as murder, but either way, somebody ends up dead."

I tried to wrap my head around that sentence. Manslaughter? So, what? They thought Hugo had killed Mason by accident? As soon as the thought came to me, I could see how it must have looked: Mason's coconut-bead necklace broken, the beads scattered across the parking lot; Mason crumpled at the base of the dumpster; Hugo passed out next to him, with wounds consistent with a fight. The chain of events, if you didn't know Hugo, must have seemed obvious: they argued; Hugo grabbed Mason's necklace; the necklace snapped; Mason stumbled back, lost his balance, and hit his head on the dumpster. An accident. A horrible accident. Manslaughter.

But I knew Hugo, and Hugo had never once gotten physical, never once been violent, not in all the years I'd known him. I shook my head.

"This is your warning, Mr. Dane," Acosta said as she turned to head back inside the house. "Next time, I'll arrest you for obstruction."

She paused, and then she drew a phone from her pocket and answered it. Her expression changed: her mouth hardened, her eyes tightened, her free hand curled into a fist. She ended the call curtly and looked at me. "I guess today's your lucky day, Mr. Dane. Your friend made bail."

CHAPTER 9

"That did not go as well as I'd hoped," Fox said when I climbed into the van.

I shook my head.

"Did you find anything?"

"Maybe. I don't know." I glanced at them. "Oh God, did the sheriff yell at you too?"

Fox grinned; it made them look younger. "I'm the darling of Hastings Rock, Dash. And I'm here innocently delivering centerpieces. Why in the world would the sheriff yell at me?"

"She did, huh?"

"Oh Lord, yes. She used the word 'impounded' seven times."

"I'm sorry, Fox."

"Don't be," Fox said with a laugh. "This is the most fun I've had in months. Where to?"

"Hemlock House, I guess. I think we need a meeting of the Last Picks."

On the way, I tried Lyda, but she didn't answer. I tried Hugo next, and he didn't pick up either. Maybe Acosta had been wrong. Or maybe they were simply still in the process of getting Hugo out of jail. What did it mean that Hugo was out on bail? Maybe it meant the evidence against him was weak. Maybe it meant a judge recognized how ridiculous the charge was.

Whatever it meant, it had to be good news—right?

But even though it was, without a doubt, good that Hugo was out on bail, I still found myself slumped against the door on the drive home. The weather in Hastings Rock was, on the whole, conducive to grumpiness, moodiness, and general sulking: rain, clouds, cold. And all of that sounded perfect for my current mood. Today, of course, had to be beautiful. The sky was still huge and bright and a lapis lazuli blue. The air smelled like wildflowers (well, and like DRAGON MUSK, which, on closer inspection, I thought maybe actually said DRAGON MUST, which was even more worrisome). With the window down and a breeze in my face, it was hard not to feel awake and alive and energized. But I dug deep and tried my hardest and managed to conjure up some doom and gloom to keep me company on the way home.

The problem wasn't that Sheriff Acosta had threatened me into staying away from the investigation. I could handle that; I understood why she did it, and all things considered, she'd done it about as nicely as anyone could expect. I liked Acosta—at least, I liked her as much as I could without knowing her. Sure, it was a small town, and we occasionally passed each other in the Keel Haul or at Rock Top Brewing (I'd never seen her at the Otter Slide). And yes, more than once she'd caught me loafing at the sheriff's office, talking with Deputy Bobby. She seemed like a good person with a difficult job. Although yes, it would have been awesome if she'd welcomed me aboard and told me how grateful she was for my sleuthing savvy. If I were Vivienne Carver, I thought, the sheriff would have been falling over herself to ask for my help.

I thought of Acosta's face and decided maybe not this particular sheriff.

No, the real problem was that if Sharian was telling the truth, then I had no idea what to do next. It was one thing for Grandma Jodi (I couldn't help thinking of her that way) to lose her temper and make a stupid—and not-so-grandmotherly—remark about killing Mason. But it was another thing entirely for her to lie to the sheriff about where she was the night Mason was killed.

But what was I going to do about it? I didn't think Fox and I could sneak into the house a second time, and I doubted Grandma Jodi would agree to talk to me, no matter what reason I came up with. And even if I did get to talk to her, what was I going to ask? Were you going to kill Mason if he tried to give away that money? Did you sneak out of the house and murder your grandson? Even if I got her to confess, what would it take to convince the sheriff—not to mention a jury—that, instead of Mason being killed in an argument with his homosexual lover, his grandmother had murdered him because she had a freaky obsession with preserving the family fortune?

When I put it like that, it didn't exactly sound airtight, but I didn't have any better theories. I kept coming back to the fact that Mason and Cole were twins. In the real world, that didn't matter, of course, but I'd been reading mystery novels for *way* too long. In one Agatha Christie novel, for example, the twist with the twins had to do with how one of the names was spelled—it looked like it might have been a typo, actually, but then it turned out to be the key to the whole thing. But I didn't know how a typo might explain why Mason had been killed. Maybe I needed to put the family trust paperwork through a spellchecker.

We were halfway up the drive to Hemlock House when I saw a familiar silhouette on the terrace. Even at a distance, there was no mistaking that swooshy hair. I sank down into the van's decrepit upholstery (hand to God, I think it was velour) and said, "Oh no."

Hugo and Millie were sitting together, talking and laughing.

As Fox was still parking the van, I jumped out and hurried toward the house.

"Dash!" Hugo said. He looked tired. Actually, he looked wrecked—dark hollows under his eyes, a hint of stubble on his jaw, a cast to his skin that suggested a point beyond exhaustion. But he smiled when he saw me, and his whole face lit up. "Millie was telling me how you're settling in."

"What are you doing here?" I asked.

"Oh my God, Dash, Hugo is AMAZING!" Millie's excitement managed to swallow even the sound of the waves for a moment. "He said I have great energy!"

"*I* told you that you have great energy," I said.

"You said she had too much energy." Fox said as they joined us. "That was the time Millie had to drag you out of bed, oh, around noon."

"Dash," Hugo murmured, but he was smiling more broadly.

"And," Millie said, "remember how you said you didn't know anything about hair? And Indira said that was okay, and I said that was okay, and Keme rolled his eyes, and Fox said, 'What kind of gay are you?'"

"I asked him that again today, actually," Fox said.

"Hold on—" I tried.

"Well, Hugo has so many good IDEAS! He told me I should try a balayage pixie, and he told Indira she should get a shag, and he told KEME—" I had a momentary thought that her breathlessness might, blessedly, prove fatal. "—he should get an earring!"

"An earring isn't a haircut," I said. "And Hugo doesn't know anything about hair."

He cleared his throat. "Uh, I know a little. I had to do some research for my next book, there's this character—"

"AND!" Millie continued (even Hugo looked a bit taken aback by that eruption), "You know how you won't go in the ocean because you're afraid of sharks?"

"I'm not afraid of sharks. I grew up by the ocean, and—"

"He had a dream," Fox told Hugo.

"Dreams mean something! And that shark was not messing around!"

"He also had a dream that he married Queen Elizabeth."

"Okay, I'm never telling any of you anything—"

"Hugo told Keme that when he moves here, he wants Keme to teach him how to surf!"

When I looked at Hugo, he gave a rueful smile and raised one shoulder.

"What is going on?" I asked. "How long was I gone? Is this a Rip van Winkle situation?"

"Are you hungry?" Hugo asked. "When was the last time you ate?"

It did seem like Indira's waffles had been hours ago, but I managed to say, "I'd like you to answer my question: what are you doing here?"

"I had to list a local address," Hugo said. "One of the conditions of my bail is that I remain in the area, and I spent pretty much everything I had to make bail. Lyda suggested Hemlock House." A little line appeared between his eyebrows. "Is that okay?"

The vision came to me of Hugo here for the foreseeable future: Hugo in the morning, Hugo in the afternoon, Hugo in the evening. Hugo talking to Fox and Indira and Keme and Millie. Hugo being his usual Hugo self, which meant charming and sweet and impossible to resist. He was like a force of nature. In a couple of months, my life would be exactly the way it had been when I'd left Providence. And then I realized this also included Hugo meeting Deputy Bobby. A laugh verging on hysteria bubbled up inside me. Hugo and West would probably be best friends.

I went inside.

"It's his blood sugar," Hugo said behind me. "It hits him hard when it drops."

"It is not my blood sugar!" But it was a little too close to a scream for comfort.

Somehow, I ended up in the kitchen, standing in front of the fridge. The cool air felt even colder against my hot face. I couldn't seem to make sense of what I was seeing, so I grabbed something at random and prayed it was cake. I didn't even make it to the table; I unwrapped the plate at the counter, grabbed a fork, and dove in.

Lemon icebox was my only clear thought as the first burst of soury-sweet hit my tongue. Thank God.

Keme appeared in the doorway to the servants' dining room.

I growled at him.

For some reason, that made him break out into a grin. He ducked his head back into the servants' dining room, and even though I couldn't hear anything, he must have said something because Indira laughed. A moment later, she followed him into the kitchen. Fox, Millie, and Hugo came into the room not long after that.

Hugo grabbed a paper towel and folded it and brought it over to me. I tried my growling trick, but he smiled and slid the folded napkin under my plate.

"How about a sandwich?" he asked. "Something with a little protein."

"We're not allowed to use the kitchen. This is Indira's space."

"I don't mind," Indira said. "Hugo knows his way around a kitchen."

I hid the shock of that betrayal behind another bite of lemon icebox cake.

"Ham and Swiss?" Hugo asked.

"I hate ham and Swiss."

"Ham and Swiss is your favorite," Hugo said, "and I'll cut it diagonally the way you like."

Millie made a sound like that was the most adorable thing in the world. Fox and Keme were pretending to hang themselves, and they were cracking each other up.

As Hugo busied himself getting the mayo and the meat and the cheese and the lettuce—okay, maybe I *was* hungry—he asked, "How's your writing going?"

"None of your business."

He winced. "Where'd you get stuck?"

"I'm not stuck."

"Hugo got a starred review for *The Mirror Box*," Millie announced.

Hugo gave her a look like that had been a secret, and Millie blushed.

"You got a starred review?" I asked around more icebox cake.

"It was a nice surprise," he said with another of those half-shrugs.

It took me about five seconds to muster the good grace to say, "That's wonderful. Congratulations."

"It's more convincing if you don't sound like you're biting your tongue in half," Fox said.

"What's *The Mirror Box* about?" Indira asked.

Hugo opened his mouth, but before he could start, I said, "I'm sorry, am I the only one who remembers that Hugo was arrested for murder? I know I'm a party pooper, but maybe that's what we should be focusing on. Life isn't all surfing and starred reviews and—and ham sandwiches."

Keme was giving me his disappointed face again.

"Let's talk about that later—" Hugo began.

And it was such a Hugo thing to say—such a maddening thing to say—that I dropped my fork and said, "No. We're going to talk about it now."

Before he could protest, I grabbed his arm and marched him out of the kitchen.

"Where are we—" he tried.

I propelled him in front of me, up the servants' stairs to the second floor. He tried to collect himself on the landing, but I chivvied and pushed and shoved until we ended up in one of the empty bedrooms. Like the rest of the house, it still had most of its original décor: damask wallpaper in a rich blue; a dresser with mirrored panels; the smell of lilac sachet and furniture polish (even though I'd had to let the housekeeper go); an oil painting of, uh, I want to say a gelding; an enormous fireplace; and, of course, the four-poster bed.

Hugo, naturally, immediately looked at the bed.

I looked at the bed again. It was approximately the size of an ocean liner.

"Are you insane?" I asked.

Hugo's grin was a little bit boyish, a little bit abashed. "I've missed you."

"We're not talking about that. We're not talking about us. We're not talking about anything except this stupid murder and how to prove that you didn't kill Mason. You didn't, did you?"

"No."

"Can you prove it?"

"How am I supposed to prove it?"

"I don't know, Hugo. I'm looking for a little help because I don't want to have an ex-boyfriend on death row."

"I don't think Oregon has the death penalty."

"Stop joking around!"

I hadn't meant to shout, but the words thundered through the room.

So much for conflict averse, a small part of my brain said.

Hugo stared at me. The good humor drained from his face, and without it, the bone-deep exhaustion was laid bare. He dropped onto a carved wooden chest, put his head in his hands, and worked fingers through that beautifully swooshy hair.

"I'm sorry," I said.

He shook his head.

After a painful eternity of agonizing over my next move, I sat on the chest. Then I put my arm around his waist. It felt like a long time before he tipped his head to rest on my shoulder.

"God," he whispered, "I'm in so much trouble."

And that was one of the things that had attracted me to Hugo in the first place: he was so smart. (Yes, and the handsomeness.) Hugo wrote crime fiction—not mysteries, by the way; crime fiction. He knew what it meant that he'd been arrested. He knew what the evidence against him meant.

"Are you okay?" I asked.

He didn't answer. And then he turned his head into my shoulder, and it was disturbing how familiar it felt, the weight and shape of his body against mine. "I am now," he said in that same whisper.

Oh no, my brain thought. No, no, no.

I stood and moved across the room.

Hugo came after me.

I kept moving until I ended up cornered next to the horse painting. Hugo leaned against the wall. The painting was the only thing separating us. There was a substantial lamp on the mantel, and I thought maybe, as a last resort, it would be my defending-my-honor lamp. My chastity lamp. He smoothed down the hair on the side of my head; his fingers bumped the side of my glasses. I jerked backward and hit something, and—because why wouldn't it?—the painting pivoted in its frame.

On the other side of the painting, a cramped, dusty wooden staircase led up.

Hugo blinked. "Is that a secret passage?"

"No," I snapped. "Don't all your horse paintings also double as doors?"

Hugo's eyebrows went up.

I tried to push the painting—well, I guess, shut, although that doesn't sound right. Back into place. It spun in a circle. I tried again. It kept spinning. I realized I probably looked like a maniac, pushing and shoving on a horse painting as it spun and spun and spun.

Hugo put his hands on my shoulder and eased me away from the wall. Something clicked, and the horse painting swiveled back to its original position.

"Hidden catch—" Hugo began.

"I know there's a hidden catch!"

The horse stared at me with a lot of judgment.

"Are you okay?" Hugo asked. "You've got your crazy eyes."

"No, I'm not okay. I'm worried about you. And I'm worried about this murder. It's weird, Hugo. It's really weird. Someone killed Mason, and they managed to do it outside a popular bar without being seen, without being heard. Mason's family is seriously messed up—and that includes the ex-bride-to-be—and there was a lot of money on the line. Even people who love each other do crazy things when it comes to money."

Hugo frowned. "You think someone in his family killed him?"

"I don't know. It wasn't a robbery gone wrong. It wasn't a gay bashing. It wasn't—" I let my voice go dry. "—an altercation with his homosexual lover."

To give him credit, Hugo did blush, but he also gave me a crooked grin that undermined it.

"There weren't a lot of people in town who knew him," I said. "I think it had to be someone he knew, someone who came to Hastings Rock with him."

"Someone who had a motive."

"Exactly."

"Well, the bride-to-be doesn't have a motive, does she? She would have wanted him alive so she could get her hands on that money—if we're assuming the money is the motive."

"See, that's what I thought," I said, "but then I talked to her—I don't know, Hugo. She's wrapped up in herself, and she's a lot savvier than she lets on. I think she's been working on Mason for a long time, trying to make sure he was her financial future. They'd had a lot of ups and downs; maybe this was the final straw, and she wanted payback for everything she'd put up with."

"I don't see it," Hugo said. "If she's savvy, why take such a risk? Why not move on with her life and find some other guy?"

"Because she wasn't planning on killing him. She was just so angry. She was furious. She hated him."

"Did she seem like she hated him?"

"Well...no."

Hugo hemmed, his expression thoughtful. It was like old times, I thought. Hugo and I fleshing out a plot. Hugo pressing me when details didn't add up. Me pushing back because they did add up, he just didn't see it. That sense of déjà vu was so strong that for a moment, I felt dizzy, and waves of hot and cold ran through me.

"Tell me about last night," I said. "What happened with Mason?"

That boyish grin was back. "Really, Dash?"

"Not that, dummy." I held up a finger. "The facts. Where did you meet him, what did you do, all of that."

"This new Dash is more assertive."

"Maybe it has something to do with being dragged into homicide investigations by idiots. Answer the question."

Hugo crinkled his eyes with amusement, but his voice was serious when he said, "Mason and I matched on Prowler last night."

"Okay."

"You know what Prowler is?"

"Of course I know what it is," I somehow managed to say. "Where were you?"

"At my hotel. I'm staying—I was staying—at the Rock On Inn, and I was..." Another hint of a blush. That one-shouldered shrug. "Lonely."

"Oh my God."

"Hey," he said with a little laugh, "I came to see you first."

"Oh my *God*, Hugo. Fast-forward through the gross parts, please."

"We met at Rock Top Brewing—have you been there?"

"Hugo!"

"Okay, okay. We got some food. Some drinks. We talked."

"How did Mason seem?"

"Up."

"Up?"

"Energetic. A little too energetic, actually."

"Like he was on something?"

"Maybe. That was what I thought at first, but then, I don't know, that didn't seem right. It was more like he was worked up. I thought maybe he was excited."

Or, I thought, he was sublimating his rage at his family and Sharian, all the emotions from a day's worth of argument, into a kind of manic enthusiasm. That seemed more likely to me.

"What did he talk about?"

"I don't know. We talked about books, of course. Music. TV. First-date stuff—"

He caught himself, but only barely.

I almost said something. I almost asked. But I had enough restraint to know I'd only upset myself; it wasn't hard to imagine the string of guys Hugo would have met after I left. Which, good for him, right? He was a kind person. He was smart. He was funny. He deserved to be happy. Back in Providence, when we would go out, there were always guys who noticed Hugo. He'd never have to spend a night alone (in a Class V haunted mansion, much less) if he didn't want to.

"That sounded bad," he said. "That's not what I meant."

I shook my head. "He didn't tell you about Sharian?"

"About his ex-fiancée?" Hugo asked. "About the wedding he'd called off literally a few hours before? No, Dash. Trust me, I'd have spotted the red flags."

"What happened next?"

"We got a little rowdy, I guess. We were drinking a lot. They asked us to settle up and leave."

"Rock Top isn't exactly a dive bar. It's mostly families."

Hugo grimaced. "I was in a bad place, and I wasn't making responsible choices."

"So, you got thrown out. What then?"

"It's a little hazy. He said he knew a place. He was—I don't know if he was getting angry, or if the anger was just starting to come out. He said they threw us out because we were gay. I tried to tell him it didn't seem like that, but I wasn't, you know, at my best. He said he knew a place. I think he drove—God, that reminds me: I have no idea where my rental is."

"We'll track it down."

"Anyway, that's about all I remember."

"You don't remember the Otter Slide?"

He shook his head.

"You don't remember seeing me?"

He groaned softly.

"Uh huh," I said with the satisfaction of every blue-hair and teetotaler and maiden aunt in the history of the world.

"Please don't judge me."

"You couldn't even stand up straight, Hugo."

"I said don't judge me!" But that half-abashed smile curled the corner of his mouth, and he shot his eyebrows up.

"So, you don't remember anything? Nothing about Penny, the fight with Cole, going out into the parking lot?"

Hugo shook his head.

"You don't happen to remember who killed Mason, do you?"

He gave me a look.

"It was worth a try," I said. "Okay, well, I guess we're back where we started."

Hugo opened his mouth to respond, and instead, he yawned.

It went on for a long time.

Like, a long time.

"Let me guess," I said. "You didn't sleep last night."

"I'm fine."

"And you're still hungover." He started to speak, and I said, "Did you ask Indira for ibuprofen?"

"I have a tiny headache."

"Get in bed."

"Dash, you're—"

"Better yet, take a shower and get in bed."

"Why don't we go downstairs, and I'll finish making you that sandwich? We can try to figure out—"

"Bed."

He made a face.

"I'll leave you some clean clothes."

"If I sleep now, I won't be able to sleep tonight."

"Oh, aren't you smart? I'll wake you up in a couple of hours."

"But—"

"Bed!"

He looked at me for a long time before murmuring, "Very assertive." And then he started taking his clothes off.

I hurried out of the room and refused to think about, consider, entertain, or, uh, think about Hugo. In any possible way. I found a clean hoodie that was usually baggy on me but would probably fit Hugo all right, and I dug around for clean joggers. I left them folded outside his room. In the distance, I could hear the shower running.

When I got downstairs, Indira, Keme, Fox, and Millie were gathered around the table in the servants' dining room. A pot of coffee and, more importantly, a coffeecake were waiting. Fox was reading something on their phone. Millie and Keme were playing fast hands. Millie was giggling uncontrollably, and Keme's grin was a white slice in his darkly tanned face. Indira had a paperback folded open—it might have been something on science or psychology, or it might have been (wait for it) *Reverse Harem Runaround* (a Reverse Harem Runaround Universe novel). You never knew with Indira.

It was hard to believe, but the light slanting past the gingham curtain was the rich gold of afternoon, and as I dropped into a seat—what I was distantly starting to realize was my seat, the way the seat near the window was Indira's, or the seat near the cellar stairs was Fox's—I said, "It's time for a nap."

"You've been awake for three hours," Fox said without looking up from their phone.

"Where's Hugo?" Millie asked, her game with Keme forgotten. "He said he wanted to see some of the jewelry I made, and then we're going to go to the farmer's market, and then he promised me he was going to show me how to make my own seaweed snacks."

Keme's smile shrank to a hard line, and his dark eyes glittered.

"God," I said, "what is wrong with him? He's facing a murder charge, and he's acting like he's on vacation."

Indira paused in the act of slicing the coffeecake. Fox looked up from their phone. Keme had a small, satisfied smile.

"Is something wrong, Dash?" Millie asked.

Yes, I wanted to say. Yes, something was wrong. He's my ex. Yes, he's charming. And yes, he's sweet. And this was all perfectly, quintessentially Hugo. Which was why everyone (except me) had fallen in love with him. It wouldn't be long before the questions started: why'd you break up? He seems so great, what happened? He's such a good guy, are you sure you can't work things out? The exact same questions I had moved to Hastings Rock to avoid. It was enough to make me want to scream until my head fell off.

Somehow, I managed not to scream. Or have my head fall off. Instead, I said, "Sorry. I'm a little tired."

"Three hours," Fox murmured.

"Well, I used a lot of energy in those three hours!"

Even Indira's eyes got a little wide at that. She, at least, understood the sensible thing to do: she passed me a plate with a slice of coffeecake, filled a mug with coffee, and said, "Why don't you eat something?"

I did. And it helped.

Keme rolled his eyes.

"What happened at the Gauthier-Meadowses' house?" Indira asked when I served myself a second slice of cake.

So, I told them: Gary's phone call and learning about his passive-aggressive mind games, the argument between Becky and Jodi, Penny rifling Mason's stuff, and then the conversation with Sharian.

"I wonder what she was doing," Millie said.

"Penny was looking for evidence," Fox said. "She killed Mason; I'm sure of it. That little stunt in the Otter Slide gave her a perfect excuse for any future DNA evidence—it's a classic case of hiding evidence with evidence."

"Oh, maybe," Millie said.

"Maybe?"

"But I was talking about Sharian. I mean, why sneak outside the house to make a phone call? And why didn't she want Dash to see her phone? I mean, she's allowed to call whoever she wants, right?"

"I'm not sure about that," I said. "I think she's toeing a pretty fine line with Jodi right now—Jodi's got everyone locked down, and even though Sharian technically doesn't have any reason to stay, she's doing whatever Jodi says. Maybe that includes keeping Mason's death quiet for now. I could see Sharian having a hard time with an order to stay off social media. The bereaved ex-bride who happens to find consolation in showing off her vocal prowess. She'd get a lot of hits, maybe get some attention for her singing career."

Keme rubbed his fingers together.

"You know what I think?" Millie said. "I think she thinks she's going to get money from Jodi if she does what Jodi wants. I mean, that's how Jodi controls everybody—that's what Sharian told you, right? Kind of like my mom with our allowance growing up." When Keme side-eyed her, she giggled and said, "Don't look at me like that!" She gave Keme a tiny shove, and although Keme glared at her and pretended to fall out of his chair, you could tell he almost died, right then and there, of pure happiness.

"What I don't understand is the inheritance or the will or the trust or whatever you call it," Indira said. "Let's assume what Sharian told you is true: she was trying to trap Mason before he got access to the trust. Mason had the jitters, but it looked like he was going to go through with the wedding, and everything was fine until he revealed he was going to give the money away. Okay, that's not exactly true love, but I don't see why she'd kill him."

"It was a rage killing," Fox said. "Spontaneous."

Indira shook her head. "And the same goes for Jodi. Even if she lied to the sheriff and left the house last night, why drive into town to kill Mason? Why not do the easier—and safer—thing and simply change the terms of the trust? That would have solved the problem."

"Rage killing," Fox said.

"You can't say everything was a rage killing."

"Fox might be right," I said. "What I saw at the Otter Slide, it looked like a fight that had gotten out of hand. And that's how the sheriff is framing the case against Hugo—she thinks Hugo and Mason argued about something, it got physical, and Mason tripped or was pushed and hit his head on the dumpster. Manslaughter, not murder."

"See?" Fox said. "Things are looking better already."

I gave them a look.

Keme nudged Millie, and Millie nodded. "But isn't she changing the trust like Indira said?"

"What?" I asked.

"Jodi. You said you overheard her talking about how it's her money and she can do whatever she wants with it. That sounds like she's changing the trust. Or changing something—something that Becky didn't like."

Indira frowned. "Becky called today and asked me to help with a small memorial service tomorrow night at the house. While I'm there, I'll keep my ears open. If Jodi did change the trust, the odds are good that they'll still be arguing about it."

"At a memorial service for a murdered boy," Fox said. "What a charming bunch."

"And I'll see if I can get anything out of Cole," I said.

"On your date."

Keme scowled.

"It's not a date," I said. "It's reconnaissance. Uh, is it reconnaissance?"

"No, dear," Indira said. "It's a date, but like in *Alias*."

Fox nodded. "That means your greatest weapon is your sexuality."

Keme whispered something to Millie, and Millie cracked up.

"This is the kind of treatment I get from my best friends," I said.

"That's sweet, dear," Indira said.

"I don't know about best," Fox said.

"His sexuality," Millie said and then dissolved into giggles.

CHAPTER 10

Being a full-time mystery writer, part-time super sleuth, and occasional, uh, wedding venue host means that sometimes it's my job to make impossible decisions.

"If I get the *al pastor*," I said, "I get all that delicious spit-grilled flavor, plus the marinade, plus it's pork."

LaLeesha was trying to fix her braid in the tiny mirror I knew she kept mounted above the food truck's service window.

"But if I get the Baja shrimp, I get shrimp. Plus they're beer battered. Plus they're fried."

She let out a heavy breath.

"Or," I said.

"You can get more than one taco, you know."

That was the problem with being a loyal customer: the staff began to take liberties.

"Well, not really. See, I'm meeting someone for dinner—"

LaLeesha's gaze snapped down to me. "Is it a date?"

"—so I don't want to ruin my appetite—"

"It's a date. Oh my God, it's a date. Sergey! Dash is going on a date!"

Sergey's answering rumble came from the truck's prep area. A moment later, he poked his head out and gave me a thumbs-up.

"Is good," Sergey told me.

"No, it's—"

"Number one boy."

"Okay, well, thank you, but—"

"Superstar."

"I don't know if I'm a superstar, exactly—"

"Turn around," LaLeesha said. "Wait, you're not wearing that, are you? Oh my God, I get it. It's a prank, right? Or one of those revenge dates? Did he ghost you? This is hilarious. Hold on, let me text Millie a picture."

I stalked off. I thought I heard laughter behind me; *et tu, Sergey?*

The boardwalk was busy tonight, the way it was every night this time of year, rain or shine (barring the occasional genuine downpour). The sky was darkening slowly, with a thin band of orange and purple on the horizon. Old-fashioned streetlights were coming on slowly. Tourists streamed around me and then, to make things interesting, abruptly stopped directly in front of me—they only seemed to have two speeds: either hurrying as fast as they could, while their excited children raced ahead of them; or rooted in place so they could take approximately a million photos of a featureless stretch of ocean or Tijohn's sand paintings or a lone hermit crab. More food trucks lined the boardwalk as far as I could see, and mixed with the saltiness of the marine air was the smell of fried twinkies and browning garlic and meat sizzling against hot steel. A balding man with a sunburnt nose was asking enthusiastically, at the service window of Spread Your Wings and Fry, to see the nutritional information for the mac-and-cheese waffle cone.

The afternoon had been surprisingly restful after I'd escaped my so-called friends. I'd gotten a nap (ignoring Fox's jibe about hibernation), and I'd woken up to a text from Cole about where we were meeting. We'd agreed on the boardwalk; I got the feeling that Cole wanted to go somewhere more private, but since he was (if only technically) a potential murderer, as well as a source in a murder investigation, I thought a public meeting with lots and lots of eyewitnesses would be ideal.

"Hey Dash!" That was Mr. Li, waving excitedly to me from his vendor tent where he sold his watercolors. "Good luck on the date!"

I groaned, waved, and tried to walk faster (tried and failed: a tourist lady zoomed in front of me and then immediately hit the brakes so she could study the rope wrapped around an otherwise unremarkable pile). Of course Mr. Li already knew. Everybody probably already knew. Because it was a small town—and because Let's Taco Bout Tacos was, let's face it, the single best dining experience for a hundred miles (because a) they're tacos, and b) LaLeesha and Sergey were geniuses)—if everyone didn't already know about my non-date, they would in approximately fifteen minutes.

What would Deputy Bobby think about that?

The question came out of nowhere, and it was so embarrassing that even though it had only been inside my head, I felt my face heat. In the first place, it didn't matter what Deputy Bobby thought. Or didn't think. If he thought about it at all, which he probably wouldn't, on account of the fact that he was my friend, that's all. And he was dating West. And we were friends. Because he was dating West (see above). And anyway, Deputy Bobby had already seen me on a date with Cole. And he and West had tried to set me up on other dates, even though I'd always turned them down because I didn't feel ready. And honestly, I was a grown man and an adult and, uh, independent? Maybe? I had every right to go on a date with whoever I wanted. Whenever I wanted. I could go on a date at six in the morning if I wanted. With a guy on a motorcycle. And we could go shoot guns or blow something up.

I didn't want to, though. That sounded terrible. No one should be awake at six in the morning, and motorcycles are so loud, and guns and blowing-up-things are even louder.

Not that Deputy Bobby would care even if I told him. He'd probably nod and smile and ask some appropriately polite question about the motorcycle. He'd probably want to know how many cylinders it had.

I could hear my own thoughts, and I was getting that scream-until-my-head-falls-off feeling again.

Fortunately, at that moment, a man popped up from behind Miss Gill's Sno-Cone cart. He saw me. Saw me staring at him. And then he dropped down out of sight again.

"You have got to be kidding me," I said under my breath.

I stayed where I was—resisting the urge to give ground even when an extended family of tourists surged toward me.

"Grandpa's not feeling well!" one of the women shouted.

Another woman shouted back, "Get him into the Hallmark store, quick!"

But I didn't yield. I didn't run. I stayed right where I was, and I watched as the man in question finally darted out from behind the Sno-Cone cart. He sprinted toward the edge of the boardwalk, crashed into Jamie Brennan's T-shirt stand, and then stumbled out of sight.

I went after him.

He was trying to hide behind a trash barrel when I found him.

"Hello, Hugo."

He looked better for having gotten a few hours' sleep, and he offered a smile as he stood. He looked like he was trying to pretend I hadn't caught him skulking behind a pile of refuse, and remarkably, he was kind of pulling it off. "Oh! Hi, Dash. I didn't see you—"

"Don't."

He swallowed.

"Why are you following me?"

"Uh."

"How are you following me?"

He didn't answer, but his eyes did slide to a spot behind me. I looked over my shoulder.

Keme, in hoodie, board shorts, and flip-flops, stood with his arms folded. He met my gaze without the slightest hint of embarrassment.

"Really?" I asked. "You too?"

He shrugged.

"How long?"

He shrugged again.

"The whole time," I said. "Perfect. At least you did a better job than this bozo."

Keme looked mildly gratified at that.

"Hey," Hugo said. "I think I should get some credit for being a good friend. He said it was dangerous and—"

I whirled around to glare at Keme. What I wanted to say—what hurt, to a surprising degree—was that I couldn't believe he'd talked to Hugo. Keme and I had been friends for months, and he'd never said a word to me. But a part of me knew that if I said those words, I'd be—well, I don't know what. Issuing an ultimatum, or a challenge, or something. And whatever it was, it would ruin our friendship. So, after another moment, I managed to swallow the words. Keme must have sensed some of it, though, because color rushed into his face. After a moment, he glanced away.

"You are unbelievable," I told him. To Hugo, I said, "You too. Both of you go home."

I made my way back to the boardwalk. Night was thickening, and a breeze ripped away the day's warmth. Even in my quilted jacket, I shivered. The chill didn't faze the tourists of course; not far off, an entire family was lined up by size like Russian nesting dolls, each one holding an ice cream cone.

Ice cream did actually sound kind of good, now that I thought about it.

Still no Cole. I checked my phone, but I didn't have any missed calls or messages. I opened up my thread with Cole and typed: *Everything okay?*

The screen dimmed and then went dark.

When I looked over my shoulder, Keme and Hugo were still there: Hugo with a mixture of defiance and worry on his face; Keme cool as a cucumber, sitting on the railing and swinging his legs.

Maybe Cole was too depressed. Maybe he'd fallen asleep. Maybe, I thought, he was high.

"I bet he changed his mind," Hugo said behind me. I whirled around to see that he and Keme had snuck up on me. He added, "That's what we both think."

Keme at least had the grace to look ashamed of himself.

"He didn't change his mind," I said.

Hugo made a big production out of looking around, scanning the crowd. "He's not here, is he?"

I didn't answer that.

"I think he was playing you," Hugo said.

"That doesn't make any sense."

"I bet he did this because he likes yanking you around."

"Hugo, will you please go home? This is important. I'm trying to help you, even though you don't seem to understand that part. If Cole shows up and you're still here, he might leave, or he might not talk to me, or—I don't know. Keme, please take him home."

Keme set his jaw and shook his head.

"See?" Hugo said. "Keme knows this isn't safe. That's why we're here: to make sure nothing bad happens to you."

"Nothing bad *is* going to happen to me. Get out of here before you ruin everything."

"If he's coming," Hugo said like someone making the ultimate, irrefutable argument, "then where is he?"

"I don't know," I snapped. And before I knew what I was doing, I started off down the boardwalk. "I guess I'll find out."

I made my way back to the Jeep. As I got behind the steering wheel, the passenger door opened, and Hugo climbed in next to me.

"What are you doing?" I asked.

"Making sure you don't get killed by your Prowler hookup."

"He's not—" Behind me, Keme got into the back seat. "No, no way. Both of you get out!"

"You're lucky you have good friends," Hugo said. "Friends who care about you and want to make sure you're safe, even when you're making irresponsible choices."

In the rearview mirror, Keme looked unbearably self-satisfied.

I tried not to scream as I pulled away from the curb.

The going was slow at first as we navigated the flocks of tourists who seemed to be under the impression that the entire town was one giant crosswalk. Every few feet, I'd have to slam on the brakes to spare some poor sap from Iowa or Missouri or Arkansas from being sent to the great corncrib in the sky. And they weren't even ashamed of it. One woman held up her hand—kind of like a cross between Mary Poppins and a crossing guard—and then waved eight little kids across the street. (Maybe there was some Von Trapp in there as well.) Another family that must have been from the shallow end of the gene pool made it halfway across the street before stopping to argue about which way they were going—every single one of them was pointing in a different direction. The man I took to be the dad was pointing down; God only knew where he thought he was going. A pair of men in matching felt campaign hats lurched out from between two parked cars and trundled out in front of us; they were trying to get autographs from a group of real, live surfers. Keme looked like he might die from secondhand embarrassment.

Eventually, though, we made it away from the water, and with every block, the tourist crowds thinned. The drive carried us down streets of homes where old Victorian stalwarts stood next to modernist jigsaws and Cape Cods mingled with 1950s-era beach bungalows. The shadows were getting thicker, and although lights were on in some of the homes, the town felt strangely deserted after we'd left behind the hub and bustle of the boardwalk.

When we got to the unmarked drive that led to the Gauthier-Meadowses' home, the sheriff's office cruiser was gone. No deputy stood guard. No formidable gate had been drawn shut. We drove up into the wooded hills, and the darkness was deeper under the firs and spruce. Colder, too. When I glanced back, Keme was hugging himself, and his face was tight.

The lights were off in the Gauthier-Meadowses' house when we reached it. No cars sat outside. Maybe they'd moved the cars into the garage, but I didn't think that was the case. I parked and stared at the house. Then I checked my phone. No message from Cole. Nothing.

I texted: *Hey, I'm a little worried. Could you let me know if you're okay?*

"You should try calling him," Hugo said.

The curtains were drawn in the windows. Had they all gone out to dinner? Had they all gone home?

"I'll do it," Hugo said.

Maybe that was it. Maybe they'd gone home, and Cole had decided it wasn't worth responding to my texts because he'd never see me again. Maybe he was embarrassed by what he'd said.

But, another part of my brain argued, he had sounded so lost. That was what I'd thought after that first, disastrous attempt at a date: that Cole had been a lost boy who had turned into a man without ever growing up.

"I can do it for you," Hugo said.

"I don't need you to call him for me."

"You hate talking to people on the phone." I didn't say anything. "Give me the phone, Dash. The sooner we get this over with, the sooner we can go home."

We, he had said.

Home, he had said.

It didn't mean anything, the rational part of my brain tried to argue. It was an expression.

I opened the door and got out of the Jeep.

"Hey, what are you—" Hugo's voice cut off with a familiar note of frustration.

I kept moving toward the house. If you'd asked me six months ago how I felt about detectives having hunches, I would have treated you to a long (and probably meandering) diatribe about how cheap a trick that was. Will Gower never had hunches. Will Gower observed things. Will Gower noticed that a light was burned out, or the front door had an unusual smudge, or that a curtain was askew. Will Gower detected.

But I wasn't Will Gower. And although I would have told you—on a bright, sunny day, in the safety of my own home—that I was a rational person, and that I wasn't superstitious in the slightest, and all the rest of that bunk, the truth was that I had a major case of the heebie-jeebies right then. And the longer I looked at that house, the worse it got. Something was wrong. And it wasn't because of a scrap of fabric caught on the downspout, and it wasn't because I could see footprints in the thick lawn, and it wasn't because of a mysterious tire track. If my experience with Vivienne Carver had taught me anything, it was to trust my gut. If I got the heebie-jeebies, then it's because there was a legitimate, heebie-jeebies inducing reason, even if I couldn't put my finger on it. Except for that one time I thought someone had broken into Hemlock House, and it turned out Fox needed some toilet paper, and Keme wanted to see if we still had any ice cream, and Millie had forgotten her bag, and Indira couldn't sleep so she decided to make a bundt cake. But that was only one time, and in my defense, they were making a lot of noise.

The closer I got to the house, the worse the feeling got. My stomach started to turn. My chest felt tight. Nothing moved behind the curtains—or nothing I could see, anyway; when I strained to listen, all I could hear was my heartbeat. Somewhere else, away from here, the sun was still going down, and night was settling in. But in the thick shadows of pine and cedar, it was already night. Shadows seemed to move every time I turned my head. The darkness made everything into an unfamiliar shape. I pulled out my phone and turned my flashlight on. Then I turned it off again. Sweat popped out on my face in hot prickles.

When I got to the front door, it was locked. I took a deep breath, and a childhood memory swam up: playing ding-dong-ditch with Josh (best friend age seven to eleven, before Josh tried to burn down his grandparents' barn). For a moment, the fear rising inside me felt familiar, like I needed to turn and sprint into the trees. I hammered on the door. Somehow, I managed not to run away.

"Nobody's home," Hugo said.

I jumped. Literally. And as my heart exploded in my chest, I said a lot of words. Short words. Versatile words. Words that conveyed my strong emotions.

"Well, I'm sorry," Hugo said when I finished.

Keme had one eyebrow raised. He actually looked kind of impressed.

"You scared me half to death!" I whispered.

"I said I'm sorry." He peered at the darkened windows. "What are we waiting for?"

Pushing past him, I started toward the side of the house. He and Keme clomped after me. When I came around the side of the house, I caught a glimpse of the long, rolling hills that flowed into the ocean. A flat sheen of gold in the distance suggested the end of the day, but everything else was lost in the gloom. I made my way toward the patio at the back of the house. And then I stopped.

Light showed in a window. And I was pretty sure, from my previous visit, I knew which one: Mason and Sharian's.

When I reached the window, I listened. My heart was still thrumming in my chest, so it was hard to tell, but I didn't think I heard anything from inside the room. With the ground steadily sloping downwards, the window here was too high for me to see into, so I grabbed the sill and pulled myself up.

Tried to pull myself up.

Keme snorted.

"This is why we were doing that new workout plan," Hugo whispered—unhelpfully, in my opinion. "Upper body strength is so important—"

"Just help me!" If a whisper can also be a scream, that's the range I was hitting.

Hugo made a stirrup of his hands, braced himself, and grunted as I stepped up.

"Okay," I said, "I don't appreciate the noises—"

I stopped.

On the other side of the window, Jodi Gauthier lay on the floor of Mason's bedroom. For a single, frozen heartbeat, I felt a mixture of terror at the possibility of being caught and a kind of embarrassed discomfort at having seen her like this. An empty glass lay on the floor next to her. She'd had too much to drink.

But she was so still. And she looked...smaller. Less. I'd seen death before, and I knew what I was seeing now. Cole and Mason's grandmother was dead.

A glance at the room showed me—well, saying it had been torn apart was a little dramatic. But it had definitely been searched: the bed pulled out from the wall, drawers left open, suitcases overturned. Clothes and toiletries lay on the floor. And the French doors had been forced: splintered wood showed where the latch had pulled free.

Movement on the other side of the French doors made me drop to the ground. Hugo opened his mouth, and I held up a hand. In Mason's room, someone was moving around. The steps were heavy and uneven. Then they moved away from us, and I thought I could hear them cross the patio.

Before I could think about it too much, I hurried after the sound. Hugo let out a strangled noise of frustration and tried to catch my arm. I slipped free and kept going. Someone had been in there with Jodi. Someone who hadn't cried out in shock, someone who hadn't tried to help her, someone who hadn't even seemed to react. When I reached the corner of the house, I slowed. And then, as carefully as I could, I risked a look.

The ambient light was enough for me to make out his features. Cole stood on the patio, shoving something into the firepit. Paper, I judged by the crinkling and rustling. He produced something long and thin in one hand, and I heard the trigger click—one of those butane grill lighters. But there was no spark, no flame. Cole swore under his breath and tried again. All he got was another of those dry clicks. He swore again and strode into the house.

Movement at the corner of my eye made me turn in time to see Keme launch himself onto the patio. He'd ditched his flip-flops, and his bare feet were less than a whisper on the tile. He sprinted toward the firepit and skidded to a stop. Paper rustled. Then the flash on his phone went off. And then again. And then a third time. He stopped and seemed to be doing something on his phone, but I couldn't tell what.

"Keme," I whispered as loudly as I dared. "Leave it."

The flash went off once more, and then Keme sprinted back toward us. Behind him, something moved in the lanai's darkness. Keme was running so fast that as he left the porch, he was airborne for a moment. It looked like he might go flying down the hill, into the stands of fir and pine. But somehow, Hugo caught him. He turned with Keme's momentum, swinging the boy in a half circle. Keme was grinning like a lunatic. And, I realized a moment later, so was Hugo.

I wanted to ask them what was wrong with them, but before I could, Cole's voice rang out: "Hey! Who's out there?"

Hugo was still holding Keme by one arm; he caught my shirt with his free hand and pulled both of us into a run. We sprinted along the side of the house. Behind us, Cole was shouting, but I couldn't make out the words over the sounds of our escape. When we reached the Jeep, I started the engine but left the lights off, and we tore down the drive.

And almost got ourselves killed.

As we came out of the drive, headlights blazed to the left. I hit the brakes. The other car hit their brakes. Through the headlights' glare, I thought maybe it was a dark sedan. Then a horn blared, and I dropped my foot on the gas. We swerved around the other car and sped away.

We had barely turned onto a residential street when sirens blared. On the street we'd left, a sheriff's office cruiser sped past, and an ambulance followed a moment later. Headed for the Gauthier-Meadowses' home, of course. Although who had called them—and why—I didn't know.

After a few more blocks, on a quiet stretch of street near the Japanese garden, I pulled over. I drooped in my seat, starting to tremble as adrenaline leaked out of me. Hugo was still grinning like a maniac. In the back seat, Keme lay on his side, shaking. It took me a moment to realize it was silent laughter.

"You're insane," I said. "Both of you."

"We're awesome," Hugo said. "Did you see when I caught Keme?"

"Did I see it? I was standing right there."

"Wasn't it awesome?"

"It was not awesome. It was—Keme, don't you dare give him five!"

Keme ignored me and slapped his hand against Hugo's.

"Both of you knock it off," I said. "We might be in serious trouble. For all we know, Cole saw us, and he's going to report us!"

"Report us for what?" Hugo asked. "He's not going to say anything, Dash. He's a murderer."

I opened my mouth to say—what?

Before I had to figure it out, my phone buzzed. Deputy Bobby's name showed on the screen, along with a photo in which he looked even more like a doofus than usual—he had his longboard under one arm, and his hair was a spiky, salt-stiff mess, and he had that enormous grin. He also had his wetsuit rolled down to his hips, which didn't hurt. I mean, I didn't even know some of those muscles existed. And yes, if you have to know, I'm perfectly aware that I'm a creep.

"Hey—" I began.

"Get over here right now."

"Uh, where? Also, hi. And why?"

Keme began frantically tugging on my sleeve.

"The Otter Slide." Deputy Bobby's voice was flat and had an unfamiliar edge to it. "I want to look you in the eye while you explain how you got these pictures."

"What pictures—" I began.

And then Keme displayed his phone. The messages were open, and a thread to Deputy Bobby (in Keme's phone, he was listed as plain old Bobby) showed a series of photos. The papers from the firepit. And I remembered Keme's slight pause, remembered him stopping to do something on his phone before taking one final photo.

"The pictures of a paternity test," Deputy Bobby said, "for Penny Vega's unborn child."

CHAPTER 11

We drove to the Otter Slide in silence. In the back seat, Keme looked miserable. Hugo must have caught the mood too because he didn't say anything. He didn't even remind me to signal as we turned into the bar's gravel lot. I parked and killed the engine.

"It's fine," I said to Keme. "You didn't do anything wrong."

It was hard to tell in the dark, but Keme's breathing suggested defensiveness defaulting into anger.

"It's okay," I said again, trying to work some conviction into my voice. I squeezed his hand. "We wouldn't have those pictures if it weren't for you. You were brave tonight, and it was smart to send them to Deputy Bobby." Then, trying for a lighter tone, I added, "Although if you risk your neck like that again without talking to me first, I'm going to lose my mind."

He tried for a glare that didn't quite land, but some of the tension seemed to drain out of his body.

"Come on," I said. "Let's go inside and get something to drink."

He was a teenager. Even in the midst of self-flagellation and what probably felt like world-ending humiliation, he was still a teenager. He paused mid-glare to crook a little look at me from over the collar of his shirt.

"A Coke, dingus. Nice try, though."

That earned me a smile—a small one.

Keme headed into the bar ahead of us, and as Hugo and I followed, Hugo asked, "What's he so upset about?"

"He's embarrassed," I said. "He's seventeen, but he thinks he's twenty-seven, and honestly, most of the time, he's so mature that it's hard to remember he's still a kid. And he—he doesn't do well when people are upset with him. And he doesn't do well when people he cares about are, I don't know, in trouble."

Hugo's silence was another question; we'd been together long enough for me to hear it.

"I don't know," I said with a shrug. "Indira says he has a rough home life, which has got to be true; I think he sleeps at her place half the time, and I honestly wouldn't be surprised if he was roughing it the other nights."

"God," Hugo said, "he's such a sweet kid, though."

I nodded.

"And you're good with him," Hugo added.

"I'm not good with him," I said. "He's my friend. Although he'd probably roll his eyes if he heard me say that."

For some reason, that made Hugo smile. The look on his face was strange—like he'd never seen me before, or like he was seeing something new. I didn't know what to say to that look, so I picked up the pace and headed into the bar.

The Otter Slide looked about the same as it had the other night. Someone (hopefully not Seely) had cleaned up the mess from Cole and Mason's scuffle, and the tables and chairs were back in order. The green-and-gold pendant lights left the right amount of shadows. I did a quick scout to see if I could find any new additions and spotted a tiny golden doodle plushie on a table near the door; the poor little guy looked like he was trying to pick up a saltshaker as big as he was. Journey was playing—"Don't Stop Believin'"—competing with the bells and chimes of the pinball machine in the back. Seely was behind the bar as usual, making conversation, and I took a deep breath and fell in love with her all over again: tonight was cheese curd night. Not just cheese curd night. Fried cheese curds. Fried pepper jack cheese curds. With marinara sauce.

Sure, maybe the crowd looked a little…thin. I did some mental math. Today was Friday, I thought. Normally on Fridays, the Otter Slide was packed. I recognized most of the faces as locals. Word had undoubtedly spread about Mason's death in the parking lot, but that had to be a coincidence—didn't it? I mean, it was one time. And it was an accident, er, maybe. More worrisome was that even though the Otter Slide was definitely more of a local place, a few tourists inevitably wandered in.

So, where were they tonight?

"Isn't that him?" Hugo asked.

It was him, although I'd apparently missed Deputy Bobby on my first sweep of the place. He sat in a booth near the back, dressed in a hoodie and joggers instead of his usual going-out attire (always something that West had picked out for him, always handsome, always looking a little too dapper for what I thought Deputy Bobby might pick on his own). Maybe it was a trick of the light, but his face was mostly lost in shadow. Keme sat opposite him, saying something (because of course he talked to Deputy Bobby and not me), but as Hugo and I approached, Keme slid out of the booth and headed for the bar.

"I said a Coke," I called after him.

He didn't look back, but I could tell he heard me and that he was grateful for the reminder. Teenagers love it when you tell them what to do.

Hugo steered me into the booth, and he slid in next to me. Deputy Bobby looked at us from his patch of shadow. He had both hands wrapped around a mostly empty pint (a seasonal Rock Top, of course). Voices mixed and mingled around us, vying with the music. The sounds of the pinball machine seemed incredibly loud.

"I wasn't trying to—" I began.

Deputy Bobby picked up his beer and killed it. For some reason, that stopped me. When he set the glass down, it thunked against the table, and he leaned forward. His eyes were bloodshot and starting to go glassy. His face was flushed. I realized I hadn't seen Deputy Bobby's face this red before, not ever; the color rode under his smooth, golden-olive complexion.

"Are you drunk?" Hugo asked.

Deputy Bobby ignored him. That glassy stare stayed on me. In a voice that was a little too loud, he asked, "What were you thinking?"

"Things kind of got out of hand—"

"No." He stopped. The pause had a kind of combativeness to it, and a charged, drunken significance that probably felt meaningful to Deputy Bobby. He was still talking too loudly. "I asked you what you were thinking. I want an explanation right now."

"I was thinking—" I began.

"You weren't. You weren't thinking. That's the problem."

"Hey, hold on."

"You were doing exactly what the sheriff told you not to do."

"I'm trying to help my friend," I said.

"You're interfering with an investigation." I opened my mouth, but he spoke over me. "You could get arrested."

"I—"

"Did you think about that? Did you think about the fact that you could get arrested?" I tried again, but he said, "You could have been killed!"

"I'm fine," I said. "Everyone's fine."

"I have to send those pictures to the sheriff. That's my job." He stared a challenge and then, with drunken belligerence, "My *job*."

"You should do whatever you need to do. I didn't know Keme was going to send them to you. I would have stopped him if I had, and I'm sorry; I'd never want to put you in that kind of situation."

Deputy Bobby made an angry noise.

"Nice friend," Hugo whispered.

"I've never seen him like this," I said back. And I hadn't. It was kind of scary, as a matter of fact.

"I won't tell her they're from you," Deputy Bobby said in what he probably thought was a conciliatory tone.

"She's probably going to figure it out anyway," I said. "But thank you."

"I won't tell her."

"Thank you. I appreciate that."

"But you have to be more careful. You can't take risks. You could have gotten hurt!"

"Here we go again," Hugo muttered.

Deputy Bobby's voice got even louder. "And going on a date with that guy?" Deputy Bobby made another of those drunken pauses. "Jeez, Dash. Come on."

People at the other tables were starting to turn. My face felt hot. "All right," I said. "I'm sorry I…I upset you, I guess. I think we should go." I looked around, trying to spot Keme, but I wasn't seeing anything as I nudged Hugo out of the booth.

"You did upset me," Deputy Bobby said, and it had the petulant hurt of a child. And then his voice changed, and he grabbed my arm. "No, no, no. Don't go. I'm sorry. Don't go!"

Lots of people were looking now. Seely was watching us, her expression flat as she shook a drink.

"Take your hand off him," Hugo said.

"It's okay," I told Hugo. I touched Deputy Bobby's hand; his skin felt hot and feverish, but maybe that was my imagination. I felt hot and feverish, but maybe that was the bar, and the trapped heat of bodies, and all those eyes.

"We're okay," Deputy Bobby announced. "It's all okay. We're friends. We're best friends!"

A woman tittered. Seely was still looking over at us, so I offered a discreet thumbs-up, and she nodded and went back to mixing drinks. Journey changed to Kansas, although I couldn't think of the name of the song, and conversations began to pick up again in fits and starts.

"Let's get out of here," Hugo said.

"Something's wrong."

"Yeah, he's drunk."

"Not drunk," Deputy Bobby informed us, but it was undermined by the fact that he was slumped against the back of the booth.

"I'm not leaving him like this," I said.

"Dash."

"Can you get us some water? And something to eat? We all need to take a minute to unwind."

Hugo's eyebrows drew together. He set his jaw.

"He's my friend," I said.

"We're friends!" Deputy Bobby announced again. That same woman laughed again.

"You're talking too loud," I told him. To Hugo, I said, "If it were me, he'd make sure I got home okay."

He had, in fact. My first time in the Otter Slide, I'd had, well, too much to drink. And Deputy Bobby hadn't exactly been a friend yet—he'd been more of a "deputy trying to convict me of a murder" kind of acquaintance. But he'd made sure I got some food in me, and he'd driven me home.

For a moment, I was sure it was going to be a fight—and with Hugo, fights had been rare. But then his mouth softened, and he offered a small smile. He ruffled my hair and kissed the side of my head before trotting off toward the bar.

"Hey," I called after him, straightening my glasses.

I didn't realize I was smiling until I glanced over at Deputy Bobby. He was still propped up against the back of the booth, but his bloodshot eyes were studying me.

"You scared me," Deputy Bobby said in a low voice.

"You're doing a little bit of scaring yourself," I said. "How much have you had to drink?"

"What if you'd gotten hurt? Are you okay?"

"I'm fine. A little embarrassed that my first real date turned out to be a potential murderer, but that's dating in the twenty-first century."

Deputy Bobby shifted in his seat, relaxing, his body loosening. He tilted his head back, as though I'd said something interesting. His eyes were the most remarkable color: a gold so deep they were almost bronze, rich and dark and gleaming. Objectively. Objectively remarkable.

"I changed my mind," I said.

Deputy Bobby's mouth quirked into a reluctant grin.

"I'm not fine. I feel awful, actually. Cole seemed like such a good guy." And he had; maybe not husband material, or even boyfriend material, but sweet and decent. I didn't like thinking of him as a murderer, especially not as someone who might kill his grandmother because—why? Because she might change the trust? Because Penny was going to have a baby, possibly his? Deputy Bobby was still looking at me, and I forced myself to say, "I mean, he was a disaster, sure. But he was sweet. And it seemed like he was lost, you know?"

That little grin came again.

"Something to share with the class?" I asked.

"You're weak for people who are disasters."

"Gee, thanks."

"It's sweet. Everything about you is sweet."

"I don't know how sweet it is. It's mostly because I'm a walking fallout zone myself."

Deputy Bobby shook his head. It felt like a long time passed before he whispered, "I think you're perfect."

It was definitely hot in here. Like, sweat soaking my shirt, my scalp stinging, face-meltingly hot in the Otter Slide. I thought about slipping off my jacket. And then I thought about sitting here with Deputy Bobby in nothing but a tee, and it was like someone opened the door on a blast furnace.

Somehow, I managed to say, "Well, I'm not. Ask Hugo. I'm sure he's prepared a list."

"What happened?" Deputy Bobby asked. "What happened? What went wrong? What happened?" And then his flush deepened, and he touched his neck and swallowed. He shook himself like he was trying to wake up. "God, I did not mean to say that. I think maybe—I think maybe—" He tried to slide toward the booth. "I should—"

My laugh surprised me, and I stuck out my leg and set my foot on the bench to keep him from leaving. "How about you sit for a few minutes? Hugo's going to bring us some water and something to eat. Then we'll see about getting you home."

"No, I have to—I shouldn't have—" He was pawing at my sneaker like it was a complicated lock. For some reason, he'd gotten fixated on the laces.

"I can talk about Hugo," I said. "I don't mind. Hey, leave my shoe alone, goofball."

Deputy Bobby gave up on the super lock. He slid down in his seat a few inches to recline against the back of the booth, and then he watched me, waiting with a kind of childlike expectation.

"Nothing *happened* happened," I said. I glanced over at the bar. Hugo and Keme were chatting (of course), and Hugo had even managed to rope Seely into short exchanges every time she passed him. He looked so confident and relaxed. His hair was still wonderfully swooshy, even at the end of a crazy day. Other people, having been charged with murder and spent the night in jail, would have been angry—justifiably so. They would have been tired. They might have been brusque and unkind. They could have been bitter. And Hugo, instead, was Hugo. "We weren't in love. I wasn't in love, I guess. I shouldn't speak for Hugo."

"He cares about you."

I nodded, still looking at Hugo. Something he said made Keme laugh—big, belly laughs that I rarely saw from the teen.

When Deputy Bobby spoke again, his voice was strained, as though he were struggling with the words. "He seems…he seems like a good guy."

"He is." Then I added, "Ask Indira, Millie, Fox, or—exhibit D—Keme. They're all in love with him."

"But you're not."

"I care about him. I love him—I do—as a friend. But I'm not in love with him. And I want that. I am so bad at relationships, so bad at being in them, so bad at knowing what's going on. And that's something I need to work on; I know that. But I also know that I want to feel more than what I feel for Hugo." I tried to smile, but it felt mangled, twisted around until it was something else. "We get one life, Deputy Bobby. And I want to be in love."

Kansas changed to something poppy, a droning piece that made me glad I didn't have any fillings.

"What if there isn't more?" Deputy Bobby asked. "What if that's all there is: you care about someone, and they're a good person, and you want what's best for them? What if the rest of it is something people made up for books and movies and Valentine's cards?"

I glanced over at Deputy Bobby, and I almost asked what was going on, why he was asking these questions. But the look on his face stopped me. The pain in his face was raw. As was the grief—a tremendous sorrow that made me ache to see it. And I wanted to ask, Where's West? And I wanted to ask, What happened?

But I didn't. I took a breath, and I said, "I don't know. At least I tried, I guess. I think I owe that to myself, to try. Maybe what I'm looking for doesn't exist. But maybe it does. I hope it does. I hope there's more."

Deputy Bobby looked at me. I didn't know what he was seeing. And I didn't know how to read what I saw in the polished bronze of his eyes. It felt like everything inside me had come apart, moved, begun to flutter with restless energy. He's drunk, I thought. And he kept looking at me, and I kept falling into those eyes, and everything inside me was trembling until I thought I was going to pass out. He's drunk, I tried again. He's drunk. Oh God, please let him be drunk.

The clink of a glass on the table made me start.

"Water for Bobby," Hugo said as he set down another glass. "And they have a summer highball I thought you'd like: a horse's neck. Isn't that lemon peel so cute? Burger and fries for the representative of law and order, and Dash, I swear to God you had better share these cheese curds or you're going to make yourself sick."

I tried a smile. It felt as mangled as the last one.

Hugo's eyebrows went up as he slid into the booth. "Okay. What'd I miss?"

"Nothing," I said.

"I don't understand," Deputy Bobby said. "You seem so good together."

"Us?" Hugo asked.

"He's had too much to drink," I said.

"We were good together," Hugo said. "I think we still could be."

"God," Deputy Bobby said. "That is so cute."

"But relationships are hard work," Hugo said, directing a look at me. "Even when you're perfect for each other. That's what you've got to remember."

"That is so freaking cute. That is adorable."

"Why don't you eat your burger—" I tried.

But Hugo's comment had opened the floodgates. "Was there something you wish you'd done?" Deputy Bobby asked. "Something you could have done different?"

Hugo rubbed his eyes. Then he took a drink of his cocktail—I didn't know what it was, but it looked sweet and fruity. One drink turned into a long drink. When he set down the glass, he said, "We're having that conversation?"

"No," I said.

"You seem like a great guy," Deputy Bobby said over me. "And Dash is—" Whatever I was, he didn't finish the sentence. "I mean, what went wrong?"

"Uh." Hugo looked at me. "I don't think that would be appropriate—"

"Nothing went wrong," I said.

Hugo grimaced.

"What does that mean?" I asked.

"Nothing."

"It didn't look like nothing."

Deputy Bobby leaned forward and barely caught himself on the table. He pointed at Hugo. "You see? Something happened."

"What went wrong, Hugo? Go on. Let's hear it."

"Why are you acting like this?" he asked.

"I don't know what that means. How am I acting?"

"You're acting like you're mad at me, and we were all getting along fine a few minutes ago. I've been nothing but nice ever since I came here. If you want to have this conversation, fine. I'd love to have this conversation with you. In private, not in front of your friend."

"Yeah, we've all been getting along fine. Everybody is getting along perfectly."

"What does that mean?"

"Tell me what went wrong."

Hugo picked up his drink and swirled it, staring into the miniature whirlpool. When he looked up, his face was drawn, his eyes wide. He set the glass down hard enough to slop some of the drink over the side. "All right. You have trust issues."

I could feel Deputy Bobby looking at me. The pinball machine was ringing and dinging, and ice clattered in glasses, and the dull, droning beat of the music had crawled behind my eyes. "You already used that one. I won't make myself vulnerable. I have trouble with intimacy."

"Well, it was a problem. I'm not going to pretend it wasn't."

"You want to talk about lack of trust? How about you showing up to check on me?"

The shock on his face melted into an ugly flush. "Excuse me?"

"You did it all the time. You did it coming here, showing up at my house all the way across the country without any warning. You always had an excuse like I wasn't answering my phone, or I forgot my lunch—"

"Because you did forget your lunch! You forgot it all the time! And I came here because I love you!" Hugo struggled like he was trying to hold back the next words, but they ripped their way free. "You want to talk about what went wrong? How about this, right here?"

Music buzzed in the silence.

"Hey," Deputy Bobby said. "Hey, stop. Hey, I'm drunk. I shouldn't have said anything. Hey Dash, I think I'm drunk."

"What's that supposed to mean?" I asked Hugo.

"This is what you do about everything," he said. "You think about it and you worry about it and you analyze it to death until everything is a red flag or a warning sign or rock-solid proof that I'm a terrible guy. Did you even consider the possibility that I was just bringing you lunch? That I loved you and wanted to take care of you and do good things for you?"

People were looking again, and I had that old, familiar feeling: like I was standing under a spotlight, like I could feel the heat of the halogen bulb, like I was about to catch on fire. Hugo felt farther away. Everything felt farther away. The other bar sounds shrank down to a background buzz.

"I...I don't know." My voice sounded small inside my own head. "Maybe we should have talked—"

"We did try to talk. I tried to talk. And you know what you did every time, Dash? You ran away, like you ran away when you came here."

My eyes stung. I found the little paper napkin that had come with my drink and tried to wipe them clear.

"There you go," Hugo said, his voice so thick I barely understood the words. "Proof I'm such a bad guy."

He crossed the bar and disappeared out the front door, and it jittered shut behind him.

"Oh God," Deputy Bobby said. It was almost a moan. "I'm sorry. I shouldn't have—I'm so sorry."

"Stay here," I said. I wasn't sure if he heard me. I couldn't hear myself. I managed to get free of the booth and stumble over to the bar. People were still staring: a guy in an Oregon State hat, his mouth hanging open; a woman with an Afro peeking over her menu; a cluster of college-age kids whispering furiously to each other as they tracked me. The weight of all that attention settled on my chest and made it hard to breathe.

When I found Keme nursing a Coke at the end of the bar, he gave me a miserable look.

"Can you—Hugo left." I fished my keys out. "He doesn't know—if you could—"

Keme took the keys and nodded. For a moment, I thought he might say something. Then he touched my shoulder and slipped around me to jog out of the bar.

"Can I settle up?" I asked Seely the next time she passed me.

She glanced over my shoulder, and I followed her gaze. Deputy Bobby was trying to extract himself from the booth, and he looked like he was going to face-plant in the process.

"Next time you're in," Seely said.

"Thanks."

"Want me to call him a ride?"

"I'll get him home."

"Good man," Seely said before drifting back down the bar to a waiting patron.

I wasn't feeling particularly good when I got back to the booth. Deputy Bobby had somehow gotten his laces caught on the table's bolted-down base. He was trying to yank himself free, grunting and saying un-Deputy Bobby-like words under his breath.

"Cool it, Maniac Magee," I said. I crawled under the table, slapped his leg a few times to make him hold still, and untangled the laces. By the time I got clear of the table, Deputy Bobby was leaning against the back of the booth—technically still standing, but Tower-of-Pisa style. His food—and his water—looked untouched. I caught his arm, and his eyes fluttered. "Okay, here we go."

A Native American woman in a Disneyland sweatshirt watched us leave. And a white guy who was trying to make an extra-long straw by inserting one straw inside another. And a woman who was so tan she looked like she'd been left to dry in the sun, her hair like old, bleached straw. Hastings Rock was a small town. How long, I wanted to know with a wild surge of amusement, before Millie heard about this?

Keme had taken the Jeep, and presumably he'd taken Hugo as well. Deputy Bobby's SUV was parked at the end of the lot. I got the keys out of his pocket and helped him into the back seat. He lay down immediately, his breathing softening. I realized I didn't know where he lived, but a quick rifle of the glove box turned up the registration and insurance paperwork with a Hastings Rock address. It was as good a place to start as any.

We drove out of the lot. The Honda Pilot was a lot quieter than the Jeep. Gravel crunched under our tires, and then even that sound faded as we eased onto the asphalt. The marine layer had moved in, and fog garlanded the trees. Branches glittered with moisture in the light from the old sodium streetlamps. For the first few blocks, a pair of blue-white headlights followed us. Then Deputy Bobby moaned, so I cracked the windows, and fresh air rushed through the SUV. It smelled like balsam and wet pavement. From somewhere came a whiff of laundry detergent—something generic, but clean and pleasant. And beer, of course. And Deputy Bobby's sweat. When I checked the rearview mirror again, the headlights were gone.

Deputy Bobby moaned again, and I reached back to pat his shoulder. "Please don't throw up. This is technically your car, but I have the feeling I'd be the one cleaning it up."

He didn't answer, but a moment later, his hand closed around mine. It wasn't a tight grip. It wasn't firm. His fingers were loose and a little greasy. I didn't think he knew what he was doing. It was easier, at least, to tell myself that. But I was painfully aware, too, of how well his hand fit mine. It was the right size. And even that slack grasp suggested the possibility of strength, although certainly not tonight. For the few months I'd been in Hastings Rock, Deputy Bobby had always been even-keeled, calm, basically unflappable. Well, something had certainly flapped him tonight. I thought about taking my hand back. It would have been the right thing to do, but I didn't.

The address on the car registration was a two-story walk-up with cedar shake siding. A fourplex, I thought. Two units up. Two units down. Older construction, in need of a good power washing and, to judge by the sagging treads, some safety repairs to the stairs. But old in a comfortable way. It wasn't hard to picture Deputy Bobby living here. It wasn't hard to picture Deputy Bobby living here with West.

A small lot behind the building had a handful of assigned spots. I parked and set to work getting Deputy Bobby out of the back seat. He didn't actively resist, but he was kind of a big lump, and it took a lot of stern talking and shaking his leg (literally) before he groaned and grumbled and started scooting. He lost his balance as soon as he tried to stand, and I caught him under the arms. He squirmed around until we were face to face. His eyes looked glassier under the lone security light than they had in the bar. His breath was soft and yeasty and honestly, not unpleasant against my cheek. He looked lost inside those burnished bronze eyes. His fingers found my nape and worked their way into my hair. Strong fingers, like I'd guessed. Almost painfully strong, with how tightly he gripped me.

"How about we get inside?" I asked, trying to hoist him up straighter. "And we'll get you to bed?"

Deputy Bobby shook his head. The security light painted a thin stripe across his heart-shaped face. His hair had fallen out of its usual perfect part, and it was hard to tell in the night, but it looked like he was flushed again. He worked his fingers against my nape again. His hand fit there too, my brain catalogued. His hand fit like it belonged there.

"Upstairs," I whispered.

He shook his head again. And then, in a drunken breath, "Can't."

"What do you mean you can't?"

Another shake of his head.

"Did West say something to you?"

"West's gone."

"He's gone? Where'd he go?"

"I like it here," Deputy Bobby said in that same voice that was barely a breath. He threaded his fingers through my hair. "I like being here. I don't want to leave."

"You don't have to leave," I said. But I remembered the tail of the argument I'd heard between them, and West's complaint. "Let's go upstairs, and you'll feel better."

"I don't want to leave." Deputy Bobby's head wobbled. "He's so mad at me."

I shushed him. He was starting to slip through my arms again, so I hoisted him up—no small feat, even though I had a few inches (and a few pounds) on him. The movement brought us closer together. His chest brushed mine. His head rocked forward until our foreheads met—a little bump, and then he stayed there. I was aware of him: the hard definition under the hoodie and joggers, the heat of him, the way his body aligned with mine. His lips were parted. He whispered, "Dash."

I thought—

I almost thought.

I remembered how he'd said in the bar, *I think you're perfect.*

If I moved a fraction of an inch to meet him. But I thought maybe I didn't even need to move. If I breathed. If I did anything.

Then I thought about West, and the fact that Deputy Bobby was drunk.

And as Hugo had pointed out, I had a tendency to overthink.

"Come on, big boy," I said, and I got him on his feet. "Let's get you home."

I'm not going to say it was easy, getting him up those narrow, rickety stairs. Especially when he kept grabbing on to me. Especially when I kept thinking about how it had felt to be touched by someone, even if it was only for a moment. Especially when Deputy Bobby put his foot between two treads and almost knocked both of us tail-over-teakettle.

But we made it to the top, and one of Deputy Bobby's keys unlocked the door. I waited for—well, I wasn't sure. I had the excessively dramatic vision of West waiting in the dark, in an armchair, with a long, Audrey Hepburn-ish cigarette. A part of me knew that wasn't likely. But it was hard to shake.

Instead, nothing.

I turned on the lights. The apartment was cute, and you could tell at a glance that it was West's space: the coffee table was reclaimed wood, the sofa was the color of raw flax, the scalloped lampshade made me think of seashells, and the ficus sat in an enormous ceramic planter that had probably cost a fortune. The kitchen must have been original, but West had found a way to make it look charmingly retro, with a bowl of lemons and a vintage stand mixer and an enameled pot on the stove (which I instinctively knew he never used to actually cook anything). Doggie bowls (food and water) had the name Kylie printed on them. But the water bowl was empty and dry, and no animal rushed to greet us.

Because Deputy Bobby was getting heavy, I unloaded him onto the sofa. Then, calling, "West?" I moved deeper into the apartment. It was a one-bedroom. The bathroom looked like it was due for a cleaning—not filthy, but lived in and regularly used. The bedroom had the same level of disorder that suggested a balance of neatness and the requirements of daily living. There were no plates that had been broken when they'd been thrown against the wall. There were no drawers hanging open, no shattered mirrors. It looked like a normal place where normal people lived. On the dresser, a photo showed Deputy Bobby and West when they'd been younger. Deputy Bobby looked like a baby, as a matter of fact, and he was grinning that big, goofy grin into the camera, with West behind him, an arm hugging Deputy Bobby around the neck. When I realized I'd picked it up, I set it down and wiped my hands on my jeans. I felt vaguely guilty. Like I'd stolen something. Or like I'd been peeping.

I picked out Deputy Bobby's pillow because one nightstand was covered in junk (hand creams, a glass of water, a box of tissues on its side, a magazine folded open—it looked like it was for interior decorating), and the other had nothing but a lamp. When I got back to the living room, he lay prone on the sofa, his face buried in the crevice at the back, and he was snoring softly. Fox would have said something about his tush, which was, uh, elevated.

I poked and prodded until he let me slide the pillow under his head. Then I sat and worked his sneakers off his feet. For someone who was allegedly gay, he had the straightest socks I'd ever seen—cheap, thin white ones, the kind you'd call athletic socks or gym socks. They were practically gray from being washed so many times, and one had a hole in the toe. I found a blanket in the hall closet and tucked him in. And then I turned off the light.

His voice came out of the darkness, muzzy with sleep and drink. "Dash?"

"I'm right here," I said. "Go back to sleep."

I could hear him moving around in the dark: sofa springs compressing and relaxing, the blanket rustling, lots of wriggling around as though he were trying to get comfortable. It was eye roll inducing, and I wished I could have shared it with Keme. Finally, he stopped, and I waited until his breathing evened out before I reached for the door.

But his voice came up again out of that dark place, so soft I had to strain to hear him. "Do you ever think you might be making a mistake?"

CHAPTER 12

I walked home.

I could have gotten a ride. I could have called Keme. Or Millie. Or Indira. Or Fox. Although, to be honest, I had second thoughts about getting in Fox's van again (DRAGON MUSK!). I was pretty sure I'd seen a headless doll rolling around in the back.

I didn't call anybody, though. I walked. The night was cool, but mild enough that I was fine in my jacket. The marine layer had thickened, and the damp felt good against the hectic flush in my cheeks. I passed a little strip of businesses—a pho restaurant (dark), a muffler shop (dark), America's Mattress of Hastings Rock (dark), and an E-Z Mart (still open). The fog refracted the light from the E-Z Mart's signage, and the red glow made it seem like the air was on fire.

Nothing had happened. I told myself that as I walked. Nothing inappropriate. Nothing bad. I'd helped my friend get home after he'd had too much to drink. He'd gotten in an argument with West, and West had left and taken the dog, and Deputy Bobby had been overserved, and I'd happened to be there. That was all.

The way he'd felt, sagging in my arms, his fingers twining through my hair.

The way his lips had parted.

The way he'd said, *Dash*.

And then my brain was off to the races. Maybe it hadn't been a fight. Maybe he and West had broken up. I mean, Deputy Bobby had said West was gone. And West took the dog. That didn't sound like a fight to me. That sounded like something more serious. Like, wouldn't you only say, *West's gone,* if you meant you'd broken up? Otherwise, you'd say, *West is out with his friends,* or *West is staying at his parents' tonight,* or—well, anything.

I could hear the frantic energy of my thoughts. It was enough to make me take a deep breath, step back. I had a mental image of Millie's eyes getting wider and wider as she listened to me.

Okay, I thought. Maybe tap the brakes.

Because Deputy Bobby hadn't said anything about breaking up. He hadn't said anything particularly, well, coherent, as a matter of fact. He'd had too much to drink, and he wasn't thinking clearly, and he was trying to communicate the basics to me: that something was wrong, that he was upset.

And he'd made how he felt perfectly clear at the end, hadn't he? *Do you ever think you might be making a mistake?*

I mean, talk about a bucketful of cold water. That question pretty much said it all: Deputy Bobby had been drunk, but not so drunk that he hadn't realized he'd been on the verge of making a huge—nay, an epic—mistake.

Me.

I'd been the mistake.

Which, fair enough. Considering my track record with men, he wasn't exactly wrong.

I could have tried to pretend the question meant something else. It would have been less embarrassing, actually, if Deputy Bobby had been asking about me and Hugo, for example. If he'd wanted to know, the way he'd been worrying the question all night, why Hugo and I hadn't worked out, or what we could have done differently, or (even though he'd been too polite to ask directly) why I wouldn't pull my head out of my butt and realize how lucky I was to have a shot with someone like Hugo.

Off in the distance, a lone car broke the night's stillness. The sound faded down the next block, and then only the slap of my steps broke the stillness. I drew in lungfuls of the air: wet grass, wet spruce, even wet Dash as the fog settled into my hair and clothes and misted my glasses. There wasn't much of a breeze—not enough to clear the air—but when it lifted, goose bumps broke out on the back of my neck.

His hand had been warm and solid and strong.

My phone vibrated, and my first, stupid thought was: Deputy Bobby. But when I checked it, the message was from Cole.

Where are you.?

I stared at the message. Then I locked the phone. As I started to pocket it, it buzzed again.

More messages from Cole.

hey

Dasj

Dash

I saw you

I knowp youw ere here

WHR ARE YOU

The sound of an engine made me glance over my shoulder. Headlights came toward me—more of those blue-white halogen brights, like the ones that had followed me and Deputy Bobby from the Otter Slide. I turned forward, blinking against the sudden brilliance, but it was too late. My night vision was ruined. I honestly didn't understand why anybody needed headlights that bright. They seemed like a hazard, actually—plenty of times when I'd been driving at night, I'd been blinded by a pair of ridiculously bright—

The engine roared behind me. Tires swished against wet pavement. Too loud. Too close. I glanced over my shoulder. The headlights rushed toward me. I stumbled sideways more out of reflex than anything else. *It's coming straight at you*, one part of my brain said. And another part of my brain could only stare in disbelief as the car swerved to follow me. The headlights grew until they swallowed up everything else, until I was blind and floating in that halogen glare.

I threw myself into the drainage ditch and landed hard in wet weeds, the ground spongy and slick beneath me. The car shot past. Its tires clipped the space where I'd been standing a moment before, and the tiny pieces of broken asphalt on the shoulder trembled and skittered. A wall of displaced air and hot exhaust crashed over me, and the growl of the engine filled my head.

And then the car was past.

I picked myself up, covered in drainage ditch ooze and the green stains of broken vegetation, in time to see it turn at the end of the block. Tires squealed as the car slid across wet pavement. No license plate. That was my only clear thought. No license plate, and since I knew jack all about cars, the best I could say was that it was a dark sedan. Then the driver straightened out the car, and it disappeared around the corner and was gone.

CHAPTER 13

A knock at my door woke me the next day.

I stirred in bed and immediately regretted it; my right side felt like it was one long, fresh bruise, and my head pounded in sympathy. After a few groans and moans, I said, "Go away. I'm dying."

"It's one in the afternoon," Indira said. "Get up, or I'm taking you to the hospital."

The room was full of dreary light, and a drizzle trickled down the windows; another coastal day of dirty-laundry clouds and cat-spit rain. I pulled the covers over my head, even though at that point it was mostly to make myself feel better. "Empty threat. You don't have a car."

"I'll ask Fox."

DRAGON MUST, I thought. Or musk. Whichever was worse.

"I'll lock the door."

"Fine," Indira said. "I guess Keme will have to eat the rest of the lemon-ricotta pancakes by himself."

I refused to respond to the injustice and outrage and general unfairness of that statement.

"Did I mention they have blueberries?" Indira said.

"One day you're going to be like me, dying in your bed," I said, "and then it will be my turn to torture you."

Her voice was already drifting away as she said, "I'll whip the mascarpone then."

After dragging my sorry, grass-and-weed-and-ooze speckled behind back to Hemlock House the night before, I'd showered and gone straight to bed. Not straight to sleep, though. I'd lain there, remembering the hot, foul air of the car rushing past me, remembering the cold blaze of the headlights, and how I'd stood there, frozen. Now I knew how deer felt—there was something paralyzing about all that steel and fiberglass rushing toward you. When I'd finally fallen asleep, my dreams had been formless, shapeless, dark places dripping with fog where I ran, even though I didn't know what I was running from.

Now, as ancient pipes glugged and clanked, I rinsed off quickly under a spray of hot water and wondered if it had been Cole in the car last night. He'd seen me at the house; that's what he'd said in the text. And last night, the way he'd acted, and Jodi's death, and the paternity test he'd burned in the fire pit—well, none of it sat right with me. But did I think that Cole, with his puppyish blend of adorable helplessness, was a killer? That he could kill not only his own brother, but also his grandmother, and then try to kill me?

I wanted to say no, but I still didn't have an answer by the time I'd dried myself off and gotten dressed.

When I got to the servants' dining room, Indira had laid out a place for me. Hot, fresh pancakes waited on the plate (lemon-ricotta with blueberry, and a mountain of whipped mascarpone on the side, plus some bonus blueberries for garnish).

There was no Keme in sight.

"Hey," I said.

"Needs must," Indira said with a smile. She poured each of us coffee from the carafe. "You had a hard night, I hear."

I paused with the fork halfway to my mouth. And then I said, "Indira, you know you don't have to do this, right? Cook stuff for me, and set the table, all that. I mean, I know we're in a weird position because of how things ended with

Vivienne, but you're welcome to stay here as long as you want—no cooking required. This was your home before it was mine."

Her eyebrows went up. She touched that white, witch's lock of hair and brushed it to the side. And then, in a voice I couldn't decipher, she said, "That's kind of you. Thank you. I enjoy cooking. And I enjoy doing things for my friends. And—" She stopped and cocked her head, and a funny smile crossed her face. "Why don't we agree that I'm a grown woman, and I'm not going to do anything I don't want to do?"

"Okay. But you don't have to."

"Do you want me to stop cooking?"

"God, no. Please. I'd starve to death. Keme too. And probably Fox, since they steal half our food."

Indira's smile looked closer to the real thing this time. "Eat your pancakes before they get cold."

They were amazing, by the way. And the whipped mascarpone? Chef's kiss.

"Millie said—" Indira began.

I groaned around a mouthful of fluffy deliciousness.

With a hint of amusement in her voice, Indira continued, "—there was an episode at the Otter Slide."

"How?" I asked. "How is she always literally the first person in this town to know everything?"

"Have you met Millie?"

"Point taken." I forked some more pancakes and hesitated. "Where's Hugo?"

"He went into town to pick up his rental car. He said something about getting some supplies."

I grimaced and ate the next few bites in silence. And then, as I murdered those pancakes, I told Indira everything: Cole and Jodi, the paternity test, Keme sending the photos to Deputy Bobby, Deputy Bobby's drunken questioning, the argument with Hugo, and the car that had tried to hit me. The only thing I left out was what had happened when I took Deputy Bobby home. In part because I knew if I told her, I'd spontaneously combust out of sheer humiliation. And in part because Deputy Bobby hadn't known what he was doing or saying, and whatever he was struggling with, it wasn't my place to share it.

"You realize Cole might have murdered his grandmother," Indira said.

"But he's...he's not a murderer. I don't know how else to say it. He's confused. He's lost. I mean, you take one look at him, and he's like a poster child for kids who grow up having everything handed to him. He doesn't have any purpose in life, doesn't have any healthy relationships, doesn't know how to take care of himself." I almost said what I'd been thinking since that first date with Cole: that I understood, in part, what it was like to have parents whose lives revolved around something other than you. In a lot of ways, Cole and I were different, but I understood that part at least. "He doesn't care about the money. Honestly, I think he'd be happier if he could convince himself to walk away from all of it."

Indira nodded, but she said, "That's the problem, though. Many people know—or believe—they'd be happier without something. But that doesn't mean they're ready to let go of it. In fact, those same people will often fight to keep things the way they are, because people are creatures of habit and routine, and change terrifies them. Cole was facing a lot of change. He might have felt like his twin was abandoning him—in more ways than one. That could have prompted an argument. And you told us that Mason and Cole had a history of arguments, fighting, that kind of thing."

"They didn't have a history of murdering each other," I grumbled.

Indira put her chin in her hand.

"Retracted," I said around a mouthful of blueberry and mascarpone.

"On top of that, it sounds like Jodi was considering changing the trust. For all of Cole's complaints about money, that might have terrified him—the money was his safety net." Indira paused as though weighing her next words. "Particularly if he needed it to continue his substance abuse."

"So, you think he did kill them. And he tried to kill me."

"I think you shouldn't close your eyes to the possibility. But about that car last night—could it have been a drunk driver? Or a distracted driver?"

I shook my head. "I've seen that before. They drive too slow. Then they speed up. They weave back and forth, or the car drifts, that kind of thing. This wasn't that. Whoever was driving that car knew exactly what they were doing, and they wanted to kill me."

Indira's brow furrowed. In a distracted voice, she asked, "If not Cole, then who?"

"God, any of them. Penny has been acting strange from the beginning. She hated Mason; she made that clear when she attacked him at the Otter Slide. And she wanted something from Mason's room."

"The paternity test results."

I nodded. "Or something she could use for another paternity test—I think that's why she was looking through his toiletry kit, like she might find hair on his hairbrush, that kind of thing. Let's say she found it and went to Jodi, and they argued—I mean, Jodi seemed pretty keen on the whole marriage and family thing. Maybe she didn't like the idea of a financial obligation to an illegitimate child."

Indira made a pained face. "Dash, Mason isn't the only possible candidate. Cole might be the father. Or, for that matter, Gary."

"Becky and Gary *are* toxic," I said. "But do you think they're that bad?"

"Do you? You've been around them. Do you think they could kill their own child?"

"I don't know. Maybe. Or maybe not on purpose—that was the sheriff's theory, remember? It was an argument that got out of hand. It's not hard to imagine Becky or Gary getting in Mason's face, picking a fight about the money, and then a push, a shove, it's a tragic accident."

"But killing Jodi would have been something else," Indira said. "Cold-blooded murder. Because she was going to change the trust."

"You should have heard Becky," I said. "Her voice when she and Jodi were arguing. She was so angry. She believes that money should be hers—like, she earned it by putting up with Jodi for this long."

"Or Gary," Indira said, "because his wife's money is his money."

"I don't know if Becky feels that way, but yeah, something like that."

Neither of us said anything. I still couldn't shake the twin thing; it seemed like it had to matter that Mason and Cole were twins, but I couldn't make it work. In one of Vivienne's books, the plot had centered on a long-lost twin. Maybe there was a long-lost triplet, but that seemed like a stretch, and nothing better came to me. The pancakes had long since been demolished, and the mascarpone was gone, and I scraped the fork across the empty plate, filling the air with its soft screech.

"Are you all right?" Indira asked softly.

"I'm fine. Well, no, actually. I'm not. I'm angry. I'm angry at whoever tried to kill me last night. I'm angry that I'm caught up in this mess. I'm angry at Hugo, even though I know it's not his fault." I stopped. "I didn't know—I mean, what he said last night—that's not how I remember it at all."

"That's usually how it is," Indira said, and although her voice was dry, there was a hint of compassion in it too. "The truth is probably somewhere in the middle, Dash."

"I guess." I heaved a breath. "Is it weird that I'm even mad at Deputy Bobby? I mean, I know he'd had too much to drink. And I know he was upset. But he was asking some personal questions, and it put me on the spot, and it put Hugo on the spot, and it made me feel...awful." And even though I couldn't say the rest of this to Indira, I was mad at him because of how his hand had felt on my nape, of the reminder of what it had been like to be touched, to have a man run his fingers through my hair, to not feel so lonely. I was mad that he'd come so close to kissing me, if that's what it had been. (In the clear light of day, it seemed even less likely.) And I was mad, if I was being honest with myself, that he *hadn't* kissed me. Although I definitely didn't want to inspect that particular packet of crazy too closely.

Indira's words broke through my thoughts. "Did you consider that maybe he wasn't asking about you and Hugo?"

"Oh, he definitely wanted to know about me and Hugo. What did you do wrong? Why didn't you fix it? What could you have done better? I don't know, Bobby. I screwed up. I'm hard to be with. In emotional geography, I'm Antarctica, and none of this is Hugo's fault because I'm terrible at relationships and he deserves someone better."

"Dash," Indira said.

It wasn't a reproach, not exactly. If anything, she sounded kind. But I heard what she hadn't said—like she was shaking some sense into me. My cheeks heated, and I said, "Sorry."

"It's all right; we're all allowed to feel sorry for ourselves. Just not too much." She paused and said, "I meant, did you consider that Bobby was trying to ask you about him and West?"

The fork clattered against my plate. I looked up.

"Oh dear," Indira murmured. "You are bad at this."

"Hey!" And then, slightly more cogently: "I didn't—but he didn't—but nobody said—" And then, in a burst of eloquence, "Who told you they were having problems?"

She looked at me.

"Okay," I said with a tiny laugh. "Small town plus Millie. Got it."

"Not Millie, dear. I've got eyes. I've got a brain. They've been together almost as long as Bobby has lived here, and they're both lovely young men. But it doesn't take a genius to start putting things together when Bobby drops by Hemlock House after a shift, or he spends a free afternoon here, or he invites you hiking on the weekends."

My face felt like it was on fire. "Deputy Bobby and I—"

"Dash," she said, and I stopped. "I'm not trying to put you on the spot. That's not the point. What I'm trying to tell you is that you did something remarkably brave: you were unhappy in a relationship, and instead of staying there, instead of choosing what was safe and familiar, you decided to fight for your happiness. Even though it was scary. Even though—and I'm speaking from personal experience—it's terrifying to leave the things that are comfortable and secure, no matter how unhappy you are. And Bobby is unhappy, Dash. I've never known him, in all the time since he moved here, to drink to excess. I don't know if he's unhappy with West because they're not the right match or if he's unhappy because they're going through a rough patch—those things happen. Everything might straighten itself out in a day or a week, and they'll be back to normal. But I don't think Bobby was asking about you and Hugo last night. I think he was asking you to help him because he's hurting and he's scared and he doesn't know what to do."

"But he's Deputy Bobby!" As soon as I heard my words, I flushed. I tried to think of how to say it differently, but the only thing I could come up with was: He's Deputy Bobby. And then I remembered how he'd looked last night. Those lost eyes.

Indira must have taken pity on me because she said, "I know. But he's also a human being. And he's confused. And, I imagine, right now he feels very much alone."

I picked up my fork and spun the tines against the plate again. The chiming was shrill, and I stopped.

"All I'm saying," Indira said, and she reached across the table to squeeze my hand, "is don't judge him too harshly."

My phone buzzed, and I pulled it out to look at it. Cole's name showed on the screen.

"Oh my God," I said and showed her the screen.

"You don't have to take it," Indira said, "if you don't want to."

I nodded. But then I answered.

"Dash?" Cole asked. His voice was gravelly, and instead of the easygoing animation I remembered, he sounded subdued.

"Hi, Cole."

Silence was broken by a rasping sound that I thought, at first, was the wind. Then I realized it was his unsteady breaths. "Can we talk?"

"We're talking right now."

His laugh was short, and it went through me like an electric charge. "I guess I deserve that. I mean in person." More of those harsh breaths came across the call. "I need to talk to someone."

Outside, the crows that nested in the sea cliffs began to caw.

"I'm sorry about those texts last night," he said, his voice even lower now. He was hard to hear over the noise of the birds. "I was in a bad place, but I shouldn't have messaged you like that."

What about trying to run me over with your car, I wanted to ask.

"I didn't stand you up," he said.

"What?"

"Dinner. I didn't stand you up. That's why you came to the house, right? I fell asleep, and when I woke up, everybody was gone."

"Cole—"

"I couldn't find my phone. I looked everywhere. Then I saw my grandma—" His voice broke. It felt like a long time before he said, "You know, right?"

"I'm sorry, Cole."

"Yeah. Me too." In the distance, the crows were going wild again. "I didn't kill her."

"I didn't think you did."

He laughed. "Come on, I know how it looked. That's what I want to talk to you about. I didn't kill her or Mason. I never would have hurt either of them."

"I believe you."

"No, you don't. But I can prove it." His breathing got a little faster. "I found something."

"What?"

"I want to show you. I want to see if you think the same thing I do."

Well, I thought, if that didn't sound like a trap, I wasn't sure what would.

"I guess I could come by your house—"

"No!" The word was sharp, and it sounded like it took a lot to buckle his voice down again when he said, "No, not the house. I'm never going back there again."

"If you have evidence, this is a conversation for the sheriff."

"No way. Not a chance. You saw how they handled things so far. They want to make me look guilty."

"What does that mean?"

After several seconds of silence, he asked, "Have you ever been to Klikamuks?"

"Yeah, a few times. Hiking." Okay, more like enthusiastic walking, but that wasn't something to quibble about with a potential killer.

"You know the first lookout?"

"Cole, I don't think—"

"I know. I promise I'd never hurt you, but—" His laugh set my teeth on edge. "—I know you can't trust me. I'll be at Klikamuks for an hour, and then I'm leaving. If you want to help your friend…"

Into the silence that came after, I said, "I'll think about it."

"One hour, Dash."

Then he disconnected.

"Call the sheriff," Indira said.

"You heard him: he's not going to talk to the sheriff."

"Well, you can't go alone."

"I'm not taking Keme," I said. "He's way too protective, and he has a seventeen-year-old's total faith that he's untouchable. And Cole would hear Millie from a mile away."

"I'll go," Indira said, setting her coffee down firmly. "You're not going by yourself."

"I don't even know if I'm going at all."

With a sniff, Indira began collecting my plate, the cups and saucers, the utensils. "Shoes and socks, dear. We only have an hour." And then, voice brightening, "I'll get my gun."

"Oh my God, do not do that."

"Shoes, Dashiell."

"Why do you have a gun in the first place?"

"And socks. Quickly."

And before I could reply, she carried the dishes into the kitchen.

As I trotted upstairs, my phone rang again. It was Deputy Bobby. I stared at the phone as it rang. And rang. And rang. And then, somehow, I managed to answer it.

"Uh, hi."

My throat locked up, and I couldn't get anything out.

A few long moments followed. In a voice that on anybody else I would have called sheepish, he mumbled, "I wasn't sure you'd answer."

For some reason, that made everything easy again. "Of course I answered."

"I wasn't sure you wanted to talk to me."

"I'll always want to talk to you."

More of that silence. They did taffy-pulling in some of the artisan candy shops in Hastings Rock, and it was like that: drawn-out, slippery, lissome moments getting longer and longer.

In a tone somewhere between disbelief and scandal, he blurted, "Did you put a blanket over me?"

A laugh eased out of me. "I didn't want you to get cold."

Deputy Bobby groaned.

"The good part was that you had your nose in the cushions and your bum in the air."

"Oh my God," he breathed.

I laughed again. "It's okay. Believe it or not, it happens to the best of us."

He groaned again, but his voice was a little stronger when he said, "I need you to be honest with me: how bad was it?"

"Uh, not very?"

"I don't believe that."

"Light to medium bad."

"Light to medium? Are you for real? What happened to 'not very?'"

The giggles caught up with me as I grabbed a pair of socks from the tallboy.

"Light to medium is a huge range," Deputy Bobby said.

"Stop being a baby," I said. And then, a little more carefully, "Are you okay?"

"I guess."

"You're hungover."

"I honestly think I'm going to die. I haven't felt like this since college. Since I was a freshman, to be specific."

"Deputy Bobby was responsible even in college," I said. "Why does that not surprise me?"

"I don't know if I'd go so far as responsible." His voice was dry, but it had a funny little edge. "My parents certainly wouldn't say that."

That seemed like too big a fish to fry for this particular conversation, so I said, "Do you want to talk about it?"

"There's nothing to talk about." But a moment later, he said, "I've been going through some stuff, I guess. But that's not an excuse for how I acted last night."

"You had a little too much to drink. You didn't burn down an orphanage."

"Light to medium bad, remember? It's kind of blurry, but I get the feeling I might have made you—" He stopped. "If I did anything out of line, I mean."

The weight of him in my arms. His hand on the back of my neck. The way his lips had parted.

His voice shattered the memory. "I kind of remember, uh, asking questions that were definitely none of my business." He waited, as though that, in itself, had been a kind of question. And then he said, "Anyway, I'm sorry. And I hope you'll forgive me."

"I want you to be happy." The words exploded out of me before I could reconsider them. "You know that, right?"

He didn't say anything, but his breath had a strange hitch in it, almost like a laugh.

"I should have said that last night," I said; the explosion kept, uh, exploding. "There are a lot of things I should have said last night. Hugo and I didn't work because I wasn't in love with him. And I don't know what you're going through, Bobby. I don't know what you're dealing with, or what you're trying to figure out. But there wasn't anything Hugo and I could have done differently. There wasn't anything we could have done to fix things. I made a mistake, thinking that something that was good enough was what I wanted. And that wasn't fair to me or to Hugo. I wanted you to hear that."

He didn't say anything, but his breathing sounded thick and wet.

"And you are an amazing person," I said. "You deserve to be happy. You don't have to settle; you owe yourself more than that. And even though change is scary, well, that's why you have friends. That's why you have people who—" I stumbled. I almost said, *People who love you.* At the last moment, I managed to change it into "—people who care about you. Because we'll be here. And we'll help you. I wish someone had told me that. I wish someone had told me that it doesn't matter if everyone in the world thinks you're happy, if everyone in the world thinks you've got the perfect life, if everyone tells you what a perfect couple you are. You have to be true to yourself; it doesn't matter what anyone else thinks."

When I finished, I gulped in air. I felt like I'd run a marathon. (Full disclosure: I have never and will never run a marathon.) I wiped sweat from my forehead. I tried to swallow my heart. I considered the fact that, when I was trying my absolute hardest to help someone I cared about, I sounded like the slogan for an inspirational yogurt. *You have to be true to yourself.* Inspirational yogurt was probably setting the bar too high. Inspirational fabric softener, maybe.

Deputy Bobby spoke, and his voice was rough, and it had that funny little edge again, the one I'd heard a few moments before. "Doesn't it, though?"

"No," I said. "It doesn't."

He was silent for a long time, but his breathing was there: labored and deep. Finally, he said, "I should—"

"I'm going to meet Cole Meadows in a murder place. And it's entirely possible he's going to kill me. Well, try to. Ideally, he won't actually kill me."

One Mississippi. Two Mississippi. Three—

"What?"

It was more of a shout than a word. I moved the phone away from my blown eardrum and switched it to the other side. "Uh, which part?"

Deputy Bobby had told me any number of times that he thought being called Deputy Bobby made him sound like a character in a kids' show. Right then, he said a lot of words that, if he had been on a kids' show, would have required an emergency cut to commercial.

"I understand you're upset," I said.

Another quick cut to commercial.

"But," I said when I had an opening, "I'm going to be super safe. Indira is coming, and she has a gun."

"Why?" he asked. "Why do you do this to me?"

"Well—"

"You realize I'm hungover, right?"

"Right, but see—"

"Where are you meeting him?"

"Klikamuks," I said, "but—"

"So help me God, Dashiell, if you set one foot past the parking lot, I will murder you myself."

"That's not very supportive."

"Do you understand me?"

"Yes, yeah, I got it."

He grumbled something that would not have made it past the public television censors.

I opened my mouth—hoping for some more inspirational, yogurty wisdom.

"I can't have one day to lie around and feel sorry for myself," Deputy Bobby said. "Next time you get into the gimlets, I'm going to drag you out of bed the next morning and make you run a five-k."

"You wouldn't dare."

"All hills," he said grimly. "There's going to be so much puking."

And with that disturbing image, he disconnected.

I thought it was an empty threat. Probably. Likely. Although Deputy Bobby wasn't given to empty threats. Or empty promises. In fact, Deputy Bobby had a terrifying propensity for doing exactly what he said he was going to do, every time, without fail. I'd seen an infomercial the other night about an old lady who fell asleep in her chair and used a can of hornet spray to ward off a burglar (no, to answer your question, I still have no idea what they were selling). I was starting to think I should invest in hornet spray.

As I went downstairs, a knock came at the front door. I stepped into the hall to see Indira peering through the glass. She glanced at me and waved frantically for me to go back and mouthed, *The sheriff.*

We both knew what that meant—as soon as Keme had sent those pictures to Deputy Bobby and Deputy Bobby oh-so-dutifully forwarded them to the sheriff, there'd been a countdown running. It had only been a matter of time before the sheriff came to interrogate—uh, interview me about the night Jodi died. And, in the process, possibly arrest me for interfering in her investigation.

Indecision twisted Indira's face, so I whispered, "Deputy Bobby's meeting me there."

With a nod, Indira waved for me to go.

As I slipped into the servants' dining room, I heard the front door open.

"Hello, Indira," the sheriff said. "I'd like to talk to Mr. Dane. I understand an 'anonymous' source was at the Gauthier-Meadowses' home last night."

I almost stayed to quibble about the pettiness of the air quotes, but instead, I sprinted across the servants' dining room and let myself out the door, and then I cut across the back of the house. The lawn gave way to the sea cliffs and the twisted, tangled hemlocks that gave the house its name, but I went as quickly as I could—well, as quickly as I dared, anyway. It only took me a couple of minutes to reach the coach house, and I sent up a silent prayer as the overhead door clattered on its track that Indira could keep the sheriff occupied for a few more minutes. As soon as I could clear the opening, I eased the Jeep forward and started for my meeting with Cole.

CHAPTER 14

When I got to Klikamuks State Park, Deputy Bobby was already there. He stood in the parking lot, arms folded across his chest, his face suggesting he was imagining fresh tortures (which he would, of course, call exercise). For someone who had planned on spending the day being hung over in bed, he looked…not terrible. I mean, if we were going with purely objective observations. His black hair was back in its perfect part. His face was clear. The burnished bronze of his eyes was, perhaps, a little bloodshot. But that might also have been because he was giving me a dirty look. He wore a lightweight rain jacket because of course he did. Meanwhile, I had no rain jacket and no umbrella. I was just proud I had on clean underwear.

When I got out of the Jeep, he said, "Where's Indira?"

"She—"

"With her gun."

I put my hands on my hips. "Okay, I feel like you're taking that out of context."

"Explain that to me. In fact, why don't you explain every single terrible decision that led to this particular moment right now?"

"I'd love to do that, even though I'm not crazy about your tone. But, since time is short, I think you should call your boss and tell her you spotted me, since

I'm pretty sure she's looking for me and she'd be super mad if you didn't, you know, tell her."

His jaw actually sagged a little. In a strangled voice, he said, "What is wrong with you?"

"I'm a people-pleaser. I don't know how to turn it off."

As Deputy Bobby took out his phone, he said several things that suggested he was not, in fact, pleased with me. Quite the contrary, actually.

I waited until he was talking to Sheriff Acosta before I jogged toward the trailhead. I made it about halfway before I heard a furious, "Dash!"

I decided to go a little faster. Cole might get spooked if I didn't have a chance to warn him I'd brought a friend.

The lot was mostly empty. There were a couple of Subarus parked at one end, and an old junker of a Chevy with a camper shell in the bed. There was also a dark Mercedes. I'd seen it before at the Gauthier-Meadowses' house, and I was pretty sure it had halogen lights.

Even mid-afternoon, the day was gloomy and dark, and the weather seemed unable to settle. When the wind picked up, raindrops spattered my face. When the wind died, the air was chill and close and damp. The dirty tin underbelly of the clouds seemed lower and darker, and they scudded inland overhead. A storm was moving in.

It was darker under the trees, but I kept to an easy jog as I started up the path. In the distance, thunder rumbled. Ferns trembled when the wind picked up again, their fronds bending under the weight of scattered raindrops. The air had the sweetness of spruce mixed with other, more pungent smells: rot and mud and a whiff of something sickly sweet—overripe blackberries that had fallen and moldered on the ground. Klikamuks, the name of the park, was from the Chinook Wawa, and it meant blackberries. The bushes covered most of the park, which was a headland jutting out into the Pacific. I was glad when the salty storm air pushed back that sickly sweet smell, even if only for a moment.

Deputy Bobby caught up with me a few hundred yards from the first lookout. I heard his steps first—their heavy, familiar plod. And then the rhythm of his breath. We'd spent enough time out on trails; it couldn't have been anybody but Deputy Bobby. He caught my arm when he got close enough and dragged me around to face him. His eyes were definitely bloodshot, but I hadn't been wrong about the dirty look either. He gave me a tiny shake like he was beyond words.

"Cole didn't want the sheriff involved," I said. "He thinks the sheriff is trying to frame him."

"That's ridiculous."

"I told you I was doing this because you're my friend and because I'd like some help. And I know you're a deputy, and you have responsibilities. But right now, Cole isn't a suspect, is he?"

"He's a person of interest."

"Fine. But unless you're going to arrest him, I want you to hang back and let me talk to him. He's scared. On the phone, he sounded terrified, actually. Do you understand?"

Deputy Bobby stared at me. "Let me make sure I got this right: you want me to stay here so you can talk to him alone."

"Yes."

"Even though he might have killed two people."

"Correct."

It looked like Deputy Bobby struggled for a long moment. Probably tamping down his more murderous impulses. Finally, he said, "And you brought me out here because I'm your friend, but I'm not supposed to do anything except hang back and let him kill you."

"Well, and avenge my death, of course. Plus—and I have to be honest, I'm a little disappointed—you usually bring an extra jacket for me."

It was something in his face. Something almost like helplessness.

"Oh my God," I said. "You did bring one? That's so sweet. I knew I should have waited."

His grip on my arm had turned into what us literary folks might have called *clutching*. As in, fingers biting in deep. Suggestive of strong feelings. Presumably because he was so happy he'd brought an extra jacket for me.

"I'll be okay," I said as I slipped free. "Trust me."

His face communicated many things in the forest's gloom. Trust was not one of them.

As I made my way up the trail, the sound of the rain thickened—the rapid drumming of droplets striking the canopy overhead. Leaves bent, branches bowed, and then the first strikes found the back of my neck as fog thickened into a drizzle. I shivered and pulled my hood up to keep my glasses clear. I could, of course, change my mind. I could call back to Deputy Bobby. He wouldn't think less of me; if anything, he'd be thrilled that I'd come to my senses. But what about Cole? Would he run? Would he shut down? Would I lose this chance—maybe my last chance—at proving Hugo's innocence?

WWWGD? What would Will Gower do? That was the real question. And I knew the answer. Whether Will Gower was a surly FBI agent or a recalcitrant private eye or a bookseller-turned-amateur sleuth, he'd take the risk.

I emerged from the trees onto the lookout point; the sound of the waves met me—hard, angry slaps against the headland's bluffs. The sky was gray, and the light was gray. There were no shadows. Everything was shadows. Ferns gave way to blackberry brambles. Brambles gave way to scrubby grass. A wire fence ran a few feet in front of the edge of the cliff, a final precaution against the lip of ground suddenly giving way, which happened more often than you'd think. It looked like the Parks Department needed to get up here; one section of the fence was broken, and the wires bobbed in the storm winds.

I didn't see Cole anywhere.

My eyes came back to the broken lengths of wire that seemed to levitate out over the drop. I thought I saw something there—something caught on the wire. The wind blew rain and sea mist into my face, speckling my glasses with water, and the spray felt icy against my exposed skin. It was enough to shock me out of that moment of paralysis. Cleaning my glasses, I crossed the lookout toward the broken section of fence. I put my glasses back on again, the wind at my back this time so I could see, and I glanced out over the edge. But I was still too far back from the edge, and the angle kept me from seeing the base of the bluff. I inched out past the fence, onto that thin lip of soil and tree roots. Closer to the edge. And then closer again. The wind screamed at my back. Below me, the base of the bluff came into view.

Cole looked small down there. He lay unmoving on a rocky stretch of beach. The tide was coming in, and even with the wind in my ear, the swell and crash of the waves dominated. When the swash rolled up to meet him, it looked for a moment like he was levitating too, like the broken wires.

"Dash!" Behind me, Deputy Bobby was coming across the lookout point. "Get back here!"

He was right, of course; Deputy Bobby was always right. But before I moved back toward safety, I grabbed one of the broken lengths of wire and pulled it to me. A piece of fabric was caught at the end, torn from a garment— a hoodie, I thought. And I'd seen the heart-shaped design of the letter. Seen the purple fabric before. P, I thought. For Penny.

CHAPTER 15

It all went the way you'd expect. Deputy Bobby dried me off and sat me in his car. He even ran the heat for me before he called the sheriff. More deputies came. Sheriff Acosta came. I braced myself for screaming, for accusations, for threats. But when she finally came to talk to me, she looked tired, her hair wet in spite of her rain jacket, and the first thing she said was "I'm so sorry."

And eventually, they let me go home.

Millie wanted to talk. Fox wanted to listen. Indira wanted me to drink hot chocolate. When I said no, Keme, bless his heart, tried to get me to play Xbox with him. I recognized their worried looks. I heard, under the rattle of the rain against the windows, the concern in their voices. But I was too tired. I went to bed and, eventually, I slept.

When I woke the next morning (eleven is still morning), the day had a cold, hard compactness. The sky was a curved steel brace, the sun was a white-hot dime, and the rain had stopped. I lay in bed for a while, thinking. In one of her books, my mom had described a character's thoughts (she was the maid to a wealthy suburban family, but she was also the mother to one of the children, with some sort of secret paid pregnancy scheme the couple had cooked up, and then at the end you find out she was the wife's sister—honestly, I can't remember how it all made sense, but it's one of Mom's best) as wild-horse thoughts. So, I lay there thinking my wild-horse thoughts, trying to herd them, trying to corral them, and then watching them all break loose again.

A rap at the door made me say, "I'm dead."

Hugo laughed quietly. And then, with a trace of uncertainty unusual for him, he asked, "Could I come in?" In a rush, he added, "To say goodbye."

"What do you mean 'goodbye'?"

The door opened, and Hugo stepped into the room. He looked like he'd gotten a better night's sleep than I had. His hair was perfectly swooshy again, and he wore a crewneck sweatshirt with shorts and somehow made it look chic instead of (as Millie had once innocently observed of yours truly) like it was time to do laundry.

"Are you okay?"

I nodded, which is an impressive feat when you're lying down.

"I didn't get a chance to say this yesterday." Hugo stopped and touched the collar of his sweatshirt. His hand dropped again. "So, I wanted to tell you before I left. Thank you, Dash. For everything. For believing me. For working so hard to make sure I didn't—" He laughed, and it sounded a little wild. "—didn't go to prison for murder, I guess. It still sounds unreal."

I grabbed my glasses to get a better look at him. "What's going on? What do you mean, you're leaving?"

"And I'm sorry about yesterday. About Cole. I know you liked him. Cared about him, I mean. I'm so sorry you had to go through that."

It was harder to shrug in bed. I sat up. I shrugged. "I guess I understood him a little. It's hard to grow up with parents who...who aren't always there."

Hugo's face softened. He sat on the edge of the bed, and the springs squeaked. "You are nothing like Cole and Mason."

"I am, though, Hugo. I mean, what am I doing? I'm living in this big, empty house. I'm playing at being a detective. I don't have a job, I don't have hobbies, I don't have—"

I managed to stop myself, but Hugo gave me a look that wasn't exactly amused but wasn't exactly…not. "A boyfriend?"

I shrugged again.

"You're being dramatic," he said. "And you're overthinking. As usual."

"Rude."

"I'm not your boyfriend anymore," he said. "I can say whatever I want."

"Hugo!"

"Are you still feeling sorry for yourself?"

"I'm not feeling sorry for myself!"

He considered me, running his hand under his chin, the soft rasp of his knuckles against a day's stubble. "Dash, can I ask you something?"

I nodded.

"What—" But he stopped. "Why? I mean, I get it. You told me how you feel. But you ran away." It was hard to separate the tangle of frustration and hurt in his voice. "You ran away from everything, and I just can't believe it was all because you broke up with me—it wasn't only because of that, anyway, was it?"

After a moment, I shook my head.

"So, why?" Hugo asked.

"Because I was afraid." The look on his face made me hurry to add, "Not of you. God, Hugo. No. I was afraid—I was afraid my life would keep being what it was. And I want more. I don't want to be Jonny and Patricia's kid. I don't want the expectations that come with that. I don't want the plans that come with that. I want to be me. I don't know what that means, I guess. Not entirely. But I want to find out."

"So." He seemed to struggle for a moment, and the words that came were hard. "I was part of the plan."

"No, Hugo. You are a wonderful person I was lucky enough to meet. And you are sweet and funny and smart and so talented. I'm so grateful for the time we had together. And I'm so happy you're in my life again, even if it's in a different way. Because I'd like to be your friend, whenever we're both ready for that. I'd like to talk to you, and pick your brain about writing, and tell you my dad's latest rant about guns. And I want to read every book you write and then email you a list of grievances."

"But I love you." He stopped and swallowed. "God, I told myself I wouldn't do this again." After a silent struggle, he said, "I know I'm not perfect, but I'll try to be, for you. We can go to therapy. Or we don't have to if you don't want to. We're so good together; please give me another chance."

It would have been easy to say yes. A part of me wanted to. Because I was lonely. And because Hugo was sweet. More importantly, he was safe. My old life was waiting like a cocoon I could crawl back into and be warm and secure. And unhappy. That, too. Terribly, desperately unhappy, even though for a long time, I hadn't been able to admit it to myself.

"I'm sorry, Hugo. What you said the other night at the Otter Slide—I don't think you're a bad person, and I'm sorry I made you feel that way. But what you're asking—I don't feel that way about you. And, if I'm being honest, I don't think you feel that way about me either. Or at least, maybe it's more complicated than you're willing to admit."

He tried for a smile, and it was awful. He let out a wet laugh. He knuckled at his eyes. "So, you've got it all figured out."

"Oh God, I don't have *anything* figured out. But I mean—Hugo, you told me you came here to get back together, and then your first night in town, you jumped on a hookup app and got blackout drunk with a guy."

"Because I missed you!"

"Hugo."

He sat still, and then he put his face in his hands.

"Am I wrong?" I asked.

It was a long time before he answered. "I don't know. I guess...I guess I've been lonely. And I was telling the truth—it was hard, how you left. How it made me feel about myself."

"I know. I should have handled that better."

But he shook his head. "No, it's okay. You're right, I think. It's easy to look back and feel like everything was perfect, even if—" He stopped, and he finished in a softer voice. "—even if it wasn't. The last few months, I kept trying to figure out how to get on with my life, but even though good things were happening— the book, the reviews, everything else going exactly the way I'd hoped—it felt like I was stuck. And then, one day, it came to me: I just had to come out here and win you back." He laughed again, more gently this time. "Look how that turned out."

"Hugo, you're a great guy. I'm sorry you're lonely now, but things will get better."

"I know, I know." But he wiped his eyes again. When he looked at me, they were shining. "This is going to sound crazy, but I'm glad this happened. I'm glad I got to see you again. I'm glad, in a weird way, I got arrested. I don't know if we would have—I don't know if we would have said some of the things we needed to say to each other. I guess I didn't know some of the stuff you were feeling. Or I didn't think about it. Didn't let myself think about it. I'm sorry for that, Dash. Because I do love you."

"I'm sorry, too. I know I'm not—I'm not an easy person to be in a relationship with. And I'm sorry that I wasn't who you wanted me to be, or I didn't feel what you wanted me to feel."

The wind was coming in hard now, rattling the shutters, shaking the glass in its frame. Hugo dried his hands on his legs. And then, fighting for a smile again, he said, "I guess that's that."

"Wait, you're really leaving?"

"I mean, why not? Talking to you helped, but I don't think you're looking for a new roommate. And the sheriff said I could go. They've got someone else in custody."

"Who? Penny?"

"Is she the friend? The maid of honor? I heard them talking about her."

"That's her." I shook my head. "God."

"You don't think it was her?"

"I don't know. I don't know what to think. It seems a little too convenient that she accidentally left a scrap of monogrammed fabric at the scene of the crime."

"Your mom would have a screaming fit if she read that in a book."

"She'd probably tell my dad to use it for target practice."

Hugo laughed. He stood, eyed me, and said, "Maybe let the professionals handle this one, Dash. I appreciate what you did; I don't think I'd be here if it weren't for you. But it's over now."

I thought about Cole. About how lost he'd been. About how he'd wanted more and hadn't known how to get it. About the drugs, and the loneliness, and his slow retreat from a world that had left him behind. I thought about how small he'd looked at the base of the cliff, the swash lifting him, the water toying with his short, messy hair. No, I hadn't seen all those details from the lookout point. But I'd seen enough, and the curse of a writer is an overactive imagination.

"You're going to be happy, you know," Hugo said abruptly. "You've got friends here who love you. And believe it or not, this house suits you. You're already changing. You're—you're more than you used to be. I don't know if that's the right way to say it, but it's true. I can see more of you. How brave you are. How determined." A smile zigzagged across his face. "You're getting surprisingly good at making decisions for someone who still can't pick which taco he's going to have. You're going to figure out who you want to be and what you want to do, and God help you if it's a job that requires you to be out of bed before noon."

A laugh burst out of me.

"And I think, Dashiell Dawson Dane, that one day, you will finish your book, and it's going to be magnificent." Hugo ducked down and kissed me on the cheek. I thought I heard him swallow. The fragrance of his aftershave, faint, took me back to Sunday mornings in our apartment in Providence, and late dinners, and bare skin. Maybe he felt it too because he gave a strained chuckle as he stepped back, and the words sounded forced as he said, "Just don't use any of the old tropes about twins, maybe." He grimaced. "Bad joke. Sorry."

"Definitely no twins."

He studied me for a moment. And then he said, "Goodbye, Dash."

"Bye, Hugo."

He let himself out the door, and his steps echoed in the stairwell, and then he was gone.

CHAPTER 16

I didn't go back to bed, thank you very much.

I did cry a little. Not because I'd changed my mind. But because it was still a loss. Even though we'd done this before, it felt...final, this time. Real in a way it hadn't before.

After a long, teary hour, though, I got in the shower, and that helped. I dressed, and that helped too. The Jigglypuff T-shirt was from Japan, and it was freaking awesome. A heavy flannel shirt and joggers blunted the worst of the day's chill. I padded downstairs in search of something to eat (no comments, please) and found Indira, Keme, Millie, and Fox in the kitchen.

"DASH!"

You get one guess who hugged me first.

My ears were still ringing as Millie gave way to Fox (whose hug consisted of a few light pats on the back before they drifted away). Indira was next, and I almost started crying again because her hugs were so good. And then, to my surprise, Keme was there, his arms stiff around me, his face set in a scowl.

"You didn't do anything wrong," I whispered. "Thank you for helping me."

Some of the stiffness melted out of him, but he was still scowling when he stepped back.

"Also," I said, "Millie got that on camera, and I'm going to have that picture printed and hang it in the hall so everyone can see the time you hugged me."

He made a rude gesture. Two of them, actually. Then he turned on Millie, who immediately began to say, "But it was so CUTE!" And then, as they began to wrestle over the phone, "No! No! Fox, help!"

"I can't," Fox said as they drifted over to a plate of another of Indira's specialties: garbage cookies. (They were not, for the record, garbage. They had M&M's and oats and chocolate chips and—well, pretty much everything. And they were amazing.)

"FOX!" Millie screamed, but it was broken up by laughter.

"You can't help?" Indira asked.

Fox shrugged. "Because I don't want to."

Indira gave them a pointed look before turning to me. "How are you doing, dear?"

"All right, I guess. Hugo and I had a talk before he left. It was—what's it called when it's absolutely terrible, but it needs to be done, and you feel better when it's over, and you're glad you did it?"

"Being an adult," Fox said drily.

"Hey!"

"In case you're wondering, the novelty wears off quickly, and then it just feels terrible."

"Don't listen to them," Indira said. "I'm sure it was hard, Dash, but you did the right thing."

"Wait, wait, wait, wait, WAIT!" Millie managed to break free from Keme—probably because Keme had a ruptured eardrum. "Hugo is GONE?"

"I didn't catch that," Fox murmured.

Indira gave them an even pointier look.

"But my mom was so excited to meet him," Millie said. "That's so unfair."

"Don't get me started," Fox said. "He was supposed to help me take a mattress to the dump."

"You two are traitors," I said. "Both of you. You know that, right?"

"My mom is obsessed with his book," Millie said. "And he's so nice."

"I've asked you the last three weekends," Fox said. "The last time, you did that horrible fake snoring to get out of it."

"And who's going to help Indira set up at the farmer's market?" Millie asked.

I looked at Indira.

She had the decency to blush. She even reached up to touch the lock of white hair before she seemed to catch herself and froze. "He volunteered—"

"Traitors!" I pointed at Keme. "And I don't even want to know. Thank God Hugo is terrible at Xbox."

"I wouldn't say he's terrible," Millie said—oblivious to Keme's not-so-subtle (and verging on frantic) hand gestures. "I watched them play for a while, and he—" She must have finally caught one of Keme's signals because her mouth stretched into an artificial smile. "He is terrible at Xbox."

"Fine," I said. "Perfect. Great. This makes my life so much easier. I'm going to live out on the cliffs and let the crows bring me food—"

"They're crows," Fox said, "not cargo planes."

I summoned my dignity and blasted Fox with a freezing look, which didn't actually seem to faze them. With that same quiet dignity, I continued, "—and Hugo can move into Hemlock House, and you can all be best friends with Hugo."

"Next time," Fox said, "try to be a little huffier. Fold your arms."

"Do you know who didn't love Hugo?" Millie said. "Deputy Bobby."

"That's because Deputy Bobby wants—" Fox managed to cut themself off at the last moment.

"Wants what?" I asked.

"Yes, Fox," Indira said, and her voice was as sharp as one of her carving knives. "Wants what?"

"Deputy Bobby," Fox said with a saccharine smile, "wants law and order and for everyone to have a respectable bedtime."

Indira shook her head.

Keme rolled his eyes.

Millie beamed.

"Nice save," I said.

"Speaking of Deputy Delicious," Fox said, "how's everything going?"

"It's a mess. I still don't know what's going on with him. West wants to move, and Deputy Bobby seems super unhappy, and I want to help him, but sometimes it feels like everything I say comes out wrong, and there's this way he has of looking at me like—" It was a little like having a fishbone catch in my throat. I sat up a little straighter and tried for a smile. And then, because I'm a wordsmith, I said, "Um."

"I meant with the case," Fox said with infinite disgust.

"Right! I don't know. Hugo said they arrested Penny, but I don't buy it. She might have killed Mason, but I can't see her killing the others. It could have been Sharian, but I can't make that line up—I think she would have either tried to talk Mason out of giving away the money, or moved on. And no matter how awful Becky and Gary seem, I can't believe they'd murder their own children."

"You haven't watched enough *Dateline*," Fox muttered.

"Maybe you could call Bobby," Indira suggested. "Since we all would like to know what's going on."

"Uh, no," I said. "I'm not doing that. I'm definitely not doing that."

"Millie," Fox said, "weren't you going to tell Bobby all your ideas for what he should get Dash for Christmas?"

"Fox," I said.

"Oh my God," Millie said. "I was!"

Fox stared straight at me as they said, "I believe there was some discussion of a teddy bear holding a heart."

"You are a monster," I said.

"Should I call him—" Millie began.

"No!" It came out a tad too...enthusiastically. "I'm calling him."

I dug out my phone, glaring at Fox the whole time, and placed the call.

Fox tried to take the phone and wouldn't let up until I placed it on speaker.

"Everything okay?" Deputy Bobby asked.

Millie made a sound like that was the most adorable thing she'd ever heard.

Deputy Bobby's silence was pronounced.

"You're on speaker," I said.

"Uh huh."

"Dash is worried about you," Millie announced. "We all are." Keme elbowed her, and she said, "Not Keme, but I think he secretly is."

"I'm actually not—" I tried.

"And Millie wanted to suggest a list of presents," Fox said. "She has observations about Dash's underwear."

"There are so many holes," Millie said like someone at the beginning of a long explanation.

"My underwear is fine," I snapped. "And it's four months until Christmas. And I do not need you yahoos—"

"I'm not sure what's happening right now," Deputy Bobby said, "but I've got to go."

"We were wondering about the case," Fox said. "If you could tell us what's going on?"

"No, I can't. It's an ongoing investigation. Goodbye."

"For heaven's sake, Bobby," Indira said, "*you* know that you don't actually believe it was that girl, and *we* know that you don't actually believe it was that girl. You don't have to put on a show for us. We're your friends."

"You too?"

A hint of color came into Indira's cheeks. "Well, we are curious, you know. And that thing about the monogrammed scrap of evidence at the crime scene, wasn't it a tad...on the nose?"

No one said anything for several long seconds.

"I feel like I have to say that some of my underwear might look, to an untrained eye, like it needs to be replaced," I said, "but the whole point of breaking in clothing—"

"Oh my God," Deputy Bobby said. The sound came of a door shutting, and in a lower voice, he said, "Look, Acosta is doing the best she can, but there's a lot to sort through. Penny argues with Mason. Mason ends up dead. Then Penny takes the paternity test to Jodi and tries to get money out of her. Jodi refuses, and she ends up dead. Cole finds the paternity test—" His voice turned dry. "—according to an unidentified witness, and then he's on the chopping block. It's not a huge stretch to imagine that Penny overheard him when he called you and said he had something important to tell you."

And something about that set the wheels in motion. Cole had called me. And I could hear Hugo saying, *don't use any of the old tropes about twins.* Cole had called me to tell me something. The old tropes about twins. Twins being mistaken for each other. A twin no one ever knew existed. The wrong twin being killed. That was usually because the twins had switched clothes at some point, usually something significant and identifying. It made me think, with a sad smile, about Cole telling me his mom had always made him wear red.

But this wasn't an Agatha Christie novel. What the sheriff needed was evidence, something that tied the killer to this crime. Like bloodstained clothes—if someone had taken something of Mason's, for example. Or DNA evidence under someone's fingernails. Heck, even dirt and rocks could be incriminating, and I found myself thinking of the loose stone I'd seen in the Gauthier-Meadowses' house. In a police procedural novel, especially one that leaned heavily into forensic science, there might be a way to analyze the gravel in the Otter Slide's parking lot. A rookie crime scene analyst might buck the system and play by his own rules and prove, beyond a shadow of a doubt, that the killer could only have picked up those tiny pieces of rock at the crime scene. (I had a brief but vivid thought that maybe Will Gower should be a hotshot dirt analyst, but I needed a more science-y name for the job. Geologist, maybe.) But the reality, I was pretty sure, was that gravel was gravel—and the fact that Gary's stupid hiking boots got the carpets dirty wasn't exactly enough to throw him in prison.

And then a thought began to form at the back of my head, something tantalizingly close that I couldn't quite put my finger on.

Cole had called to tell me something.

No, that wasn't quite right.

"But I don't understand," Fox was saying. "Why wait? And how did she know Cole had seen the paternity test? And wouldn't it be more likely he was trying to help her? I mean, he did destroy that piece of evidence. And—"

"He didn't call to tell me something," I said.

Everyone stopped.

After a heartbeat, Deputy Bobby said, "I thought—"

"He wanted to show me something."

Deputy Bobby's breathing changed. Paper rustled.

"He had something on him," Millie said. "He had something he was going to show Dash."

Keme shook his head, and Indira pointed at him as though he'd spoken. "But the killer would have taken it."

"Unless Cole fell, and the killer didn't have time to retrieve it," Fox said.

When Deputy Bobby spoke again, his voice was tight, and it sounded like he was reading. "Sneakers, joggers, hoodie, watch. Right pocket: wallet, three joints, lighter. Left pocket: keys, necklace. Was he hiding it? Maybe the sole of his shoe? Inside one of the joints?" The sound came of a door opening, and a muffled voice spoke, and Deputy Bobby said, "Coming right now." Then he added, "I've got to go," and disconnected.

I shook my head. Whatever it was, either it had been lost in the fall, or the killer had—

"Oh my God," I said. "Twins."

"What does that mean?" Indira said.

"It was in his pocket."

Fox's eyes were bright, and they spoke a little too quickly, humor edged with excitement. "I've seen this before. Dash, do you smell toast?"

I didn't even bother with a glare; Will Gower let that kind of nonsense roll right off him. Instead, in my most authoritative voice, I said, "I know who killed Cole. I know who killed all of them."

CHAPTER 17

It was late afternoon when the car finally left the Gauthier-Meadowses' house. From a distance, it was hard to make out more than a pair of silhouettes in the front seats, but I was sure it was them: Becky and Gary, finally leaving the house. Penny was in jail, and with Jodi gone, I was pretty sure Sharian had packed up and left. That meant, in theory, the house was empty.

From our stakeout spot on the side of the road—inside Fox's van, with DRAGON MUST and oceans of tulle and what looked like a woman's bra painted with a bullseye on each cup, on and on like that—we held our collective breath. But the car didn't stop or turn back, and a moment later, it went around the corner and out of sight. I opened the door.

Keme started to follow.

Millie unbuckled herself.

Fox picked up a switchblade (it was actually a toy comb, by the way—which felt about right).

"I'm coming with you," Indira said.

"We already talked about this," I said. "You're all staying here. And you're going to keep watch. And if they come back, you're going to cause a huge distraction. I'm sure you'll come up with something."

"Swan wedding," Fox said and pressed the switchblade's button. The comb shot out of its hiding spot. "I've been trying to think of a way to use that tulle for years."

"For years—" But I stopped myself. Keme was reaching for the door, clearly under the impression that he was still coming. "No! You're staying here and making sure they're safe."

Keme glared, but after a moment, he slumped in his seat.

"Indira, don't you dare use that gun. Which, by the way, I can see in your purse."

Indira gave me a frosty look and adjusted the purse on her lap.

"I can come," Millie said. "I don't have a gun or a comb or anything, but I'm SUPER sneaky."

Dear God, I thought. Somehow, I managed to say, "No, you're staying here because you and Indira are the only ones who can actually make Keme do something he doesn't want to do."

Keme made one of his favorite gestures again.

"Text me if you see anything," I said.

Fox was still trying to reset their switch, uh, comb as I got out of the van.

I jogged up the hill to the house, and the distant sounds of traffic faded as I moved away from the road. The house's concrete shell gleamed in the sunlight, but the windows were dark. I had seen the car leave, I reminded myself. The house would be empty.

After giving the front door a quick try—hey, optimism never killed anyone—I circled around back. The front door had been locked, but the doors to the lanai opened easily (for some reason, plenty of people assume locking the front door means the house is secure). The glass panes rattled softly in their frames. A moment later I was standing inside the combined family room and kitchen. The lights were off, and the shadows seemed almost total as my eyes tried to adjust to the gloom. A faint smell of microwaved curry hung in the air— burned curry. It made the hairs on the back of my neck stand up.

I made my way to Gary and Becky's room, the soles of my sneakers whispering against the floorboards. Like the rest of the house, their room was done in shades of gray and white and sandy browns, with blue accents. They had a canopy bed without curtains, a floor mirror with a rubbed-bronze frame, a rubber plant, and a pair of modernist chairs that looked curvy and soft and like they would still somehow be uncomfortable to sit in. A picture window looked out on the wooded hills and, beyond them, the slate-green chop of the Pacific.

When I opened the closet door, something squeaked. I stopped. I listened. I didn't hear anything. I checked my phone, but I didn't have any missed calls or messages. I sent up a little prayer that the Last Picks hadn't gotten distracted by their own distraction. (What in the world was a swan wedding? Probably, knowing Fox, exactly what it sounded like.)

I knelt on the closet floor, pushing aside the hanging clothes to give myself room to work, and looked at the rows of shoes. Then I began picking up each one. It didn't take long; I found it on my third try. A pair of hiking shoes. A coconut bead was caught in the thick tread next to a few tiny pieces of gravel.

Men's hiking shoes.

This—or something like this—was what Cole had wanted to show me. That's why he'd wanted to meet. That's why he'd been carrying the coconut-bead necklace in his pocket, instead of wearing it. It was a match to the one Mason had been wearing the night he died. The necklace that had broken when Mason had been killed. And here, lodged in the treads of this shoe, was the evidence that someone had been at the scene of the crime. Someone who had lied to the police about where he'd been.

I took out my phone to snap a picture.

Movement at the corner of my eye made me turn.

"I thought you might come back," Gary said. He filled the doorway as he aimed a gun at me. "I guess I was right."

CHAPTER 18

Gary didn't look good. His donut of mousy hair was sticking up in back. His face was drawn. The hand with the gun was trembling. Somewhere, he'd found a long, plastic raincoat. It must have been hot because his face was red and sweaty. For the blood, a part of me thought. That's why he was wearing the raincoat. He was already planning on the blood.

"Come on," he said. "Get out of there."

"You killed—"

"Yeah, yeah. I killed them. I killed Mason. I killed that—" He said a word that you definitely aren't supposed to say anymore. "—Jodi. And I killed Cole."

"Because—"

"Because of the money!" The hand with the gun dipped. He was breathing hard. "Because of that stupid money!"

"You—"

"She wasn't going to give us any of it. Can you believe that? The old bag said we didn't need it; Becky made plenty of money, and we owned everything outright. It was all going to Mason and Cole. After all these years. Everything I put up with from Becky. Being treated like a servant. Worse—being treated like a buffoon. I couldn't do anything right. Making fun of me to her friends. Making fun of me to the boys. Making me the butt of all her stupid jokes.

Because she knew I couldn't leave." He shook his head. "But it was all going to be worth it."

"Until Mason said he was going to give away the money. Then you—"

"I went crazy!"

"Okay, but if I could finish one sentence—"

"I went out of my mind. They were going to get everything, and Mason was going to give half of it away. I couldn't—I couldn't!" The color leached from his face until he looked gray. "Jodi and Becky had gone to bed. Sharian was drinking herself silly; she was acting like it was the end of the world, you know, because the wedding was canceled. And Penny—well, Penny was out of her mind. She didn't even notice when I followed her into town. She was too angry because Mason had knocked her up, and he *still* didn't want anything to do with her."

"Which you knew—"

"Because I found the paternity test—"

"Come on," I said, unable to help my note of frustration.

"—back in Portland. Cole helped her, you know. Mason wouldn't consent to a paternity test, not without a court order—and rightly so—but Cole, well, Cole was always a soft touch."

"And because they're twins—"

"Identical twins, exactly. That was all Penny needed—proof, if you want to call it that, that Mason was the father of her child. She wasn't stupid enough to try to use it before the wedding, though. She was going to wait."

"But you found it first, didn't you? And then Mason made his announcement about giving away the money, and you had bigger things to worry about."

Gary blinked at me as though he'd forgotten I was there. "It was an accident. It was a terrible accident. I wanted to talk to him, that's all. I had to make him understand. I'd worked for that money. I'd earned it. If he didn't want it, well, it ought to have been mine anyway. He'd had too much to drink. We argued. I wanted to—I wanted to shake some sense into him. I grabbed that stupid necklace, and it broke. He fell." In an empty voice, he said, "He hit his head."

"And Hugo was right there, unconscious, the perfect fall guy."

Gary shuddered, and with his free hand, he dry-washed his face. "It was an accident. And I knew it wouldn't help anybody—wouldn't make it any better—if I stayed. I drove home. Jodi and Becky were still asleep. I thought I saw Sharian, but when I came inside, she and Penny were asleep."

I shook my head. "She saw you. She made a mistake—one dark sedan looks like another, and she assumed it was Jodi, since Jodi—"

"She lost her mind. She went out of her head. First, with Mason. And then—and then everything. She was going to lock it all up in a trust for charity. Nobody was going to get it—nobody was going to get anything. Mason would have wanted it that way, she said. Ha! And she wouldn't talk about it, she wouldn't listen to reason. She was going to sign the papers as soon as we got back to the city."

"But you weren't going to let that happen. So, you—"

"I drugged her drink! Yes! And then I put that stupid paternity test in there. That would have been the end of it—Penny had already made a scene at the bar, and now the sheriff would see she had a motive. But my idiot son had to ruin everything. He couldn't have the decency to get high and pass out like he did every other night of his life. And then, when we were coming home, I was in the car with Becky. We almost hit you as you and your friends were leaving. That's when I knew you were still poking around."

"So, you tried to—

"I tried to run you over."

I said a few of my own not-so-polite words.

"But you got away from me," Gary said, "and before I could try again—"

The stop was so sudden and absolute that I thought, for a moment, something had happened to him. His face was washed out, a sickly white that was almost green, and his eyes looked like paper-punch holes.

"Before you could try again," I said, "you realized Cole suspected. Or maybe he knew. And then Cole had to go."

Gary dry-washed his face again.

"He wasn't soft," I said. "And he wasn't stupid. He was hurting. And he was lost. And he wanted to be more than what he was; he just didn't know how."

Rough, rasping breaths came back to me in answer. And then, voice almost unrecognizable, Gary said, "Get up."

I started to rise. And then I threw one of the hiking shoes at his face.

Gary shouted and flinched. The movement carried him backward, out of the doorway. The hand with the gun rose into the air as he tried to catch his balance, and then the gun went off. The sound was enormous in that cramped space. Chunks of plaster rained down, and gritty dust mixed with gun smoke to cloud the air.

As Gary tried to recover his balance, I darted through the doorway. He shouted. I kept running. The door to the hallway stood open, and I sprinted toward the front of the house. Gary shouted again, and another clap of gunfire chased after me. On my next breath, I tasted gunpowder and sweat and the powdery bitterness of broken drywall.

When I reached the living room, I turned—and my momentum carried me into a careening slide as I tried to orient myself toward the front door. The gun barked again. A bullet punched through the wall ahead of me, dislodging a shelf, and decorative seashells fell to shatter against the floor. I put on the gas. Broken bits of shell crunched underfoot as I barreled down the hallway. The front door seemed to balloon ahead of me, getting bigger with every step. Somewhere behind me, Gary was screaming.

I had to get outside. I had to get outside, and then I had to get down the hill, and then Fox would be waiting with the van—

But a part of me knew I'd never make it. There was too much open ground between here and there. And Gary only had to hit me once.

I threw open the door and stumbled outside.

A voice shouted, "Down!"

A familiar voice.

Deputy Bobby's voice.

I threw myself to the ground. Concrete scraped my cheek, pleasantly cool against the flush of adrenaline. The air smelled clean, like pine sap and wet duff and asphalt washed clean by rain. My chest heaved as my body demanded more air.

"Drop it! Drop it! Get on the floor!"

A thud came—the sound of a body hitting tile. Steps moved. A familiar snick—handcuffs locking in place.

And then a hand on the back of my neck. It felt exactly like I remembered.

"You're okay," Deputy Bobby said. And then, his voice rough, "You're okay."

CHAPTER 19

Expectations to the contrary, Sheriff Acosta didn't murder me. I like to think that it was because she was so grateful, but the truth was probably that she didn't want to clean up another mess. Deputy Bobby was slightly more gracious. He only used the word stupid once. He did explain, however, why my so-called friends hadn't managed to warn me: they'd never seen anyone come back to the house, because Gary had never left. He'd stayed behind when Becky went out, and when I'd started my search, he'd heard me. I decided to forgive this lapse in judgment because the Last Picks had saved my life by immediately confessing everything to Deputy Bobby when he called to, quote, "make sure Dash wasn't doing anything stupid." Which was how he'd gotten there in time to save my life.

After the dust settled, I went home, ate as many tamales as Indira would let me have, and slept.

I woke way too early the next day (nine o'clock!), but I couldn't go back to sleep. I lay there, listening to the ocean, the wind, the now-familiar sounds of an old house. When I got up and opened the curtains, a few clouds marred the horizon, like the sky was a chipped plate stamped with gulls. I showered. I checked the sky. The gulls were still there, skating along the chipped edge. I found a pair of joggers and a hoodie. Sailors used to say—I'd heard this, growing up in a port town—that the cries of gulls were the cries of dead men.

A knock came at the front door as I reached the hall, and I padded over to open it. Becky stood there, her hair pulled back into its usual severe ponytail, in a camelhair coat and business-forward shoes. The good looks that spas had maintained were cracked now. Her eyes were red rimmed and hollow. Behind her, Sharian and Penny looked like they were auditioning for the role of two wicked stepsisters.

"Mr. Dane," Becky said in a stretched-out voice and then pushed her way inside.

We ended up in the den, which felt a little grounding: the leather wingback chairs, the stately volumes lining the built-in shelves, yet another cavernous fireplace. And, of course, this room had a secret passage—just in case, say, I needed to make my escape. Becky sat. Penny sat. Sharian drifted over to the window, where the morning sun was coming in. It fell over her in a broad, golden beam. It might have been a conscious choice, but I thought it was probably more like how a cat sees a box and immediately has to sit in it.

"I wanted to thank you for your help," Becky said, opening her purse. She drew out a check and handed it to me.

"Mrs. Meadows, I can't—"

"For the venue. Of course, I owe you more than that. The sheriff is reluctant to say so, but I understand that without your assistance—" She stopped there, and her fingers curled around the arms of the chair until the leather dimpled and creaked. I heard what she might have said, though: *My son might still be alive.* Finally, in that awful, stretched-out voice, she managed, "—things would not be resolved."

"I'm so sorry," I said. "I didn't know Mason or your mother, but I knew Cole, a little. He was a sweet, sensitive person. I'm sorry about all of it."

Becky stared at me. Through me, really, because I didn't think she was seeing me. When she spoke, her voice was detached, and I thought maybe I was hearing the businesswoman who ran a multimillion-dollar corporation and had kept her family in line with an iron fist. "I should have ended things a long time ago. Gary and I were never—" She stopped again. Her hands opened and closed around the arm of the chair, where her nails had left indentations in the leather. "I should have ended things. Do you know what's funny, Mr. Dane?"

The silence lasted until I shook my head.

"I was afraid, if I did, I would lose my sons." She offered a terrible smile. And then she left.

With a downcast look, Penny hurried after her—pausing only long enough to mumble, "Thank you."

And then Sharian and I were alone.

"She thinks Becky's going to take care of her," Sharian said as she perched on the windowsill. The rich light made a golden collar around her neck. "Because of the baby. So, she's playing nice. And Becky's playing nice. They talk about the baby. Nobody talks about how Penny cheated with my fiancé. Or how she attacked him because he wouldn't acknowledge the baby. Or how it was all headed for a lawsuit." She smoothed her sundress—a white, summery thing that seemed like too little for today, for this, for right now. "Of course, I think Becky's going to take care of me too. At least for a little while. And we're not talking about how Mason and I fought. About how we'd called off the wedding. At the funeral, I'll still be his fiancée. They're having tryouts for *The Voice* in January, and Becky already said she'd book me a hotel."

Motes of dust drifted in the thick sunlight.

"I guess everything worked out, then," I said.

She kissed me on the cheek on her way out.

I left the check on the table in the servants' dining room and went to wash my face.

When I got back, the check was gone, and Indira was setting a place for me.

"You don't have to do that," I said.

She gave me a look and kept going. "I put the check somewhere safe. You can have it when I know you're not going to do anything silly."

I sat at the table and propped my head in my hands.

Indira set the spoon in its place, the way she always did, even if I didn't need a spoon. And then she did something she hadn't done before: she combed the hair back from my forehead. My eyes stung, and I closed them. Her touch was light, the motions repetitive and calming.

"I made a blueberry-oat breakfast cake," Indira finally said as her hand stilled. "And you need some protein."

"Thank you," I said. "Really. But I'm actually not hungry."

I tried to read in the living room—I couldn't get past the first page; I didn't even know what book I'd picked up. I tried to go for a walk, but I didn't even get so far as my shoes. I remembered the first time I'd seen Fox, they'd been lying on the floor in the hall. That's where I ended up, staring at the plaster ceiling and the electrolier and the spider webs that I couldn't reach even with a broom. And then I closed my eyes for a minute.

When I, uh, opened my eyes again, the shadows had shifted and deepened, and aside from the crick in my neck and a lot of fresh aches from lying on the floor, I still felt like I was in that halfway place between sleeping and waking.

It didn't even seem strange when Fox's face floated into view above mine. "What's going on down there?"

"Oh, you know," I said. "Just living my best life."

"I do know. I do indeed."

Keme appeared next to Fox. He glowered down at me. And then he kicked me—and it wasn't a cute little nudge, either. In the butt, if you have to know.

"Hiya, chief!" That was Millie, her freckles crinkling as she smiled down at me from Fox's other side. "Did you fall down or something?"

"Did he fall down for six hours?" Fox asked.

"What's going on?" I asked. "Did Indira send up the Bat Signal? Do we even have a Bat Signal?"

"We have a group chat," Fox said.

"Keme found your high school yearbook photo," Millie announced. "Dash, you were so CUTE!"

Keme looked way too pleased with himself. So pleased, in fact, that he decided to treat himself to kicking me again.

"Get up, Dash," Fox said. "That's my spot, in the first place. And in the second place, you're too young to be full of despair. And in the third place, if you're going to be full of despair, the best place to do it is on a couch while you binge a docuseries about a cult while eating an entire pan of Reese's Pieces blondies. As a side note, that's also an excellent opportunity to think about all the ways your life went wrong."

At that point, I decided to close my eyes.

At least, until Keme kicked me again.

"Get up," Fox said again. "Keme is worried about you."

"Worried about me? I'm going to need a hip replacement."

"He wants to play games with you. You should play Pong. Do they still have Pong?"

"What is happening?" I moaned.

"Come on," Millie said, and she took my arm and helped me to my feet. I got up mostly because Keme was clearly looking for another reason to kick me. Millie wrapped her hand around mine and led me toward the stairs. "I've got a great idea."

Millie's great idea, it turned out, was to play dress-up with me like I was an adult-sized (and gloomy) doll. She'd pick out an outfit for me, and then she'd send me into the bathroom to change, and then I'd come out and "model" the clothes—which meant standing there while Millie gave helpful suggestions like "Turn around" or "Do that thing with your arms," or "Smile, but like you're on that show Fox loves—Fox, what's that show called?"

"*Harlots*," Fox informed us.

"And I call this Dash's Sunday-but-I-forgot-it-was-Sunday-and-did-I-sleep-in-these-clothes-or-do-they-just-magically-look-rumpled look," Millie announced. She was digging deep now, since most of my clothes were joggers, hoodies, and gaming tees. Fox had long since gotten interested in their phone, and Keme, who was lying on a cedar chest, was grinning uncontrollably. "Oh my God!" It was the sound of genius striking. "We should braid his HAIR!"

Keme laughed so hard he rolled off the chest.

I was saved by grace—while Millie started to look up instructions on how to braid short hair ("LOTS of braids" was a phrase that kept popping out of her mouth), my phone buzzed. Deputy Bobby's name showed on the screen.

"Whatever it is, I'll do it," I said. "Rescue a cat from a tree. Save an orphan from a burning building. Rescue a cat from a burning tree. Did I mention I'd do whatever?"

Deputy Bobby's laugh was quiet and...well, on anyone else, I would have said nervous. "Hello."

"It's an emergency, you say? I'm on my way."

I could hear the smile in his voice when he said, "How are you doing?"

"Great. Do you want me to stick my head in a woodchipper or something?"

"Indira said you were...having a hard day. I'm sorry I couldn't call earlier; there's been a lot going on."

"Are you okay?"

"I'm great."

Which was such a Deputy Bobby answer that it made me want to—to bite a goose. I don't know. Is that an expression? (A consideration, every writer knows, for revision.)

"Wait," I said. "You're on that group chat?"

His silence lasted a beat too long.

"Oh my God."

"What I want to know about the yearbook picture—"

"Oh my God!"

"—is if you were trying to be funny. Or did you actually wear a fedora to school?"

"Goodbye. Good luck. I'm off to take advantage of the nearest cliff, which is literally in my backyard."

I got more of that quiet laughter, and it sounded a little less nervous this time.

"I know this is short notice," Deputy Bobby said, "but I was wondering if you wanted to come over."

"I can't. I have to braid my hair."

"So many BRAIDS!" Millie agreed.

"Yes, God, please," I said. "I'm on my way. I'm already dressed because Millie and I have been playing dolls. I'm the doll."

"I have no idea what that means."

"I know. See you soon."

When I disconnected, Millie and Keme and Fox were staring at me. They traded a look. They stared at me again.

"Dash," Fox said.

"I don't want to hear it," I said as I sprinted toward the door. "I'm fine. I'm great. I'm so much better. Thank you, uh, for whatever this was."

"Wait—" Fox tried.

By then, I was already taking the stairs two at a time. I pulled on my sneakers and ran to the coach house, and a minute later, I was on my bike (a gift from Deputy Bobby), riding into town.

When I got to Deputy Bobby's apartment, the street was lined with cars. One of the neighbors must have been having a party, which my nose confirmed when I leaned the bike against the side of the building—the smell of hot coals and mesquite and grilled meat met me, and music with a steady, thudding bass line was playing nearby.

Play it cool, I told myself. He invited you to come over. He might be feeling lonely. Maybe he needs a friend, and you're his friend, and so it makes sense that he'd call you.

As I made my way around the back of Deputy Bobby's apartment building, the music grew even louder. People filled the small lot —men and women, most of them around my age, most of them holding drinks. The smell of grilling was stronger. It took me a moment to process that the party was here—happening at Deputy Bobby's building. The realization sent a weird thrill through me. Maybe Deputy Bobby didn't want to go to the party alone. Maybe he wanted me to go with him. He'd introduce me to his friends, and I'd have to explain how we knew each other—he wanted to arrest me—and everybody would laugh.

Part of my brain was trying to tell me to slow down. Part of my brain was trying to tell me to pump the brakes.

I passed the people spilling out onto the drive and made my way to the back lot. A rap song I didn't recognize was ending, and something poppy—but moody—came on. I thought it might be Selena Gomez. And then I saw the banner: CONGRATULATIONS, WEST AND BOBBY!

I took another step. And then another. And then I stopped. The music was too loud. The beat felt off, like I couldn't quite catch the rhythm—or like another, stronger rhythm was pounding through my body.

Congratulations.

Not just congratulations.

Congratulations, West and Bobby! With an exclamation point.

I started to turn around when a familiar voice shouted, "Dash!" West, pink cheeked and beautiful, broke away from a group of young men—to judge by the way they eyed me, dissected me, and dismissed me, these were West's friends, not Deputy Bobby's. In one hand, West held a champagne flute. He stumbled once on his way over, and he burst into a delighted laugh as he recovered his balance. When he reached me, he wrapped his arms around me in a hug, and then he stepped back and held up his hand to show off a gold band set with diamonds.

"We're getting married!" West screamed. He fell against me again, arms around my neck, the sweetness of the champagne on his breath as it brushed my cheek. "Oh my God, we're getting married!"

It was another long moment before my body seemed my own again. Then I pressed a hand to his back and managed to say, "Congratulations."

"You've got to help me—" He swayed as he stepped back. "You've got to— you've got to help me pick out an apartment. You've got to help me." To a passerby, West said, "Dash is going to help me pick out an apartment."

The young woman smiled at me and kept walking.

"You're moving?" I couldn't hear my own voice, but I thought that's what I said.

"Portland." West grabbed my arm like he might slide right out of his espadrilles. "Maybe Seattle, but right now, Bobby is stuck on Portland. You can talk to him. You can tell him Seattle—" He swayed again. "You can tell him."

I nodded. I said something. Fortune or fate or chance released me—West spotted someone across the lot, let out an excited scream, and hurried away from me. I managed to get myself headed back to the street, but I barely made it to the front of the building when I had to stop and lean against the wall. The volume of the party had dropped, and instead, there was a rushing noise inside my head. The shake siding bit into my back and, at the same time, it felt soft, almost spongy. I covered my face with my hands; my cheeks were hot, and I thought I could still smell West's champagne.

Running footsteps beat the pavement. The old panic—of being seen, of being caught—surged up inside me, and I dropped my hands and wiped my face. I was straightening my hoodie when Deputy Bobby ran past me. He stopped. Turned. Looked at me.

For a single moment, pain etched his face. Pain, and shame, and what I wanted to call desperation—because I had the sense that Deputy Bobby was desperately trying to stay in control. And then he set his jaw, and he narrowed his eyes, and his look was...belligerent. An invitation to a fight. A challenge.

That made it easier. Because that wasn't Deputy Bobby, not really. The dusk softened the hard lines of his face and body, blurred the combativeness of his expression. The day was gold bleeding into black. I remembered—and my eyes stung again, for a different reason this time—what Indira had said. I could see it then, and I wondered how I hadn't been able to see it before. The confusion. The loneliness. The fear.

I managed a smile and, out of some place inside myself, I brought up words. "Hey! Congratulations!"

His eyes softened first. Then his mouth. He folded his arms and studied me. "Are you okay?" Maybe he heard how that sounded because he almost tripped over his tongue adding, "Why are you over there?"

I crossed the pavement. The music changed again, but I focused on the sound of my steps. Deputy Bobby shifted his weight like he wanted to move back, but he stayed where he was. "You know me," I said. "Crowds. I, uh, got a little overwhelmed."

Maybe it was the dark descending. Maybe that was why it seemed like the iron in his expression yielded by degrees, and I thought I saw the real Deputy Bobby. My Deputy Bobby.

"Are you okay?" he asked again. The same. Different.

I couldn't keep the smile, but I nodded.

His voice was small when he said, "I didn't know how to tell you."

There was so much packed into that sentence. More than I knew how to deal with. But I understood enough of it, I thought. Or maybe I felt it. I knew what it felt like, after all. That was why I'd stayed with Hugo so long.

When I hugged him, he dropped his arms and stiffened, and it felt like a long time before some of the tension in his body relaxed. He put his arms awkwardly around me. He smelled clean and masculine—his deodorant or his aftershave, something that probably had the word *sport* in the name. I could hear his heartbeat.

"Congratulations," I said again. "I'm so happy for you."

He gave a funny little laugh, and his arms tightened around me, and his voice had an unfamiliar huskiness when he asked, "Yeah?"

For a moment, I thought he might ask more.

But the moment passed. In the distance, fireworks popped. Light bloomed, driving away the shadows between us for an instant. And then the light died again.

"Of course," I said as I let him go. "You're my friend."

DOOM MAGNET

Keep reading for a sneak preview of *Doom Magnet*, the next book in The Last Picks.

CHAPTER 1

"Bobby!" Millie screamed. "Over HERE!"

"Okay," Fox said. "I don't think now is the time—"

"Keme! Keme! Look! *Hi!*"

"Millie," Indira said, "they need to concentrate."

Torn between distracting her friends and, well, the thrill of simultaneously cheering/screaming at them, Millie settled for hopping up and down silently, waving her arms.

It was a bright October day, the weekend before Halloween. The sky was blue. The sun was warm. And although it was cooler than the summer months in Hastings Rock, on a day like today, you couldn't really tell.

Ketling Beach was a long, wave-smoothed crescent. To the north, Klikamuks Head jutted out into the sea. South, the shoreline curved inward, and across the bay rose the dollhouse profile of Hastings Rock. Where the light caught the wet sand of the beach at exactly the right angle, it looked sheeted in silver.

Banners hung everywhere, announcing the GREMLINS AND GROMMETS SURF CHALLENGE. In smaller type, the banners explained, *Brought to you by Gremlins and Grommets Surf Camp.* The event had brought out what looked like most of the town, and people lined the beach in folding chairs, many of them wrapped in blankets and carrying thermoses of coffee. Not exactly your Malibu beach scene, but I had learned—to my surprise—that not only did the Oregon Coast have some great surfing spots, the best time of year was late October. Which seemed like a wonderful recipe for death by hypothermia.

But if the cold water had deterred anyone, you couldn't tell by the number of surfers waiting to compete. Beyond the barrier that marked the end of the spectator zone, they ran the gamut from children with foamboards (presumably the gremlins and grommets, although I wasn't entirely sure of the lingo) to middle-aged men and women who looked scarily fit for their age. (This from a guy who prefers an elevator to stairs even when he's going down.)

Deputy Bobby and Keme were down there too. They were both wearing wetsuits as they did some light cardio, warming up for the day's events. If I had to make a list of terrible, awful, horrible ways to spend the day, watching Deputy Bobby jog and do jumping jacks and laugh at something Keme said probably wouldn't rank high on the list. It might not even make the list at all.

Although, to be fair, sitting next to Deputy Bobby's boyfriend, West, probably *would* make the list. In part, that was because I was doubly self-conscious every time I looked at Deputy Bobby. (Not that I was doing anything wrong. Not that I couldn't look at him. Because we were friends, right? And friends looked at each other all the time. Even when friends were in wetsuits, and you could see all their muscles, and friends were bending and stretching and—we're just friends!) And in part, because the juxtaposition wasn't ideal. I mean, West was gorgeous. He had flaxen hair in a messy part, perfectly pink cheeks, kissably pouty lips (at least, I assumed Deputy Bobby thought they were kissable), and eyes the exact same color as the sky this morning. He was wearing a ring on his left hand these days, so I guess I needed to start thinking of him as Deputy Bobby's fiancé. In keeping with the Halloween theme, he'd chosen to go as a very, very, very (need I go on?) sexy construction worker: hardhat rakishly cocked, hi-vis vest, jean shorts, steel-toed boots. And that, ladies and gentlemen, was all. If it were me, I would have been freezing, but since West also apparently had the metabolism of a hummingbird, he looked perfectly comfortable.

Everyone was dressed up, not just West, although nobody else, as far as I could see, had gone for the pouty-sexy-where's-my-metal-clipboard look, which should have been ridiculous, but honestly? He was totally pulling it off. Indira, of course, had kept her costume tasteful. I'd asked if she was going to be a witch, and she'd asked me why I thought that, and I'd immediately regretted every life choice I'd ever made. (Answer: it's because of that lock of white hair she has, which gives some seriously witchy vibes.) Instead, she'd gone for a tweed jacket over a rust-colored sweater and jeans, which looked like a normal outfit for her. She'd added big glasses and a crumpled deerstalker cap that sat cockeyed on her head, and when I'd finally had to ask who she was, she'd said Professor Trelawney. (Which, point for me because I had totally guessed witch.)

With Fox, it was hard to tell if it was a costume or daily wear, since Fox's outfits seemed to straddle the delicate intersection of Victorian train conductor, circus impresario, mortician, and steampunk enthusiast. Today, for example, they were wearing a knee-length frock coat over a Led Zeppelin tee, plus a top hat. (Hats were apparently a thing this Halloween.) Like I said, it was hard to tell if this outfit had been plucked from Fox's daily rotation or was a Halloween treat.

Millie, on the other hand, was definitely in costume. Millie's usual attire (which consisted of cute sweaters and jeans) had been replaced by a full '80s exercise getup: a violently pink leotard, turquoise tights, and electric yellow legwarmers and sweatbands. She'd done a full blowout on her hair and looked a little like Farrah Fawcett if she'd been struck by lightning. God bless her, she'd even found ankle weights. And the thing was…Millie looked amazing. I wasn't sure she even knew how good she looked because, well, she was Millie. But I knew one thing: I was dying to see Keme's face when the poor boy finally got a look at her.

As for me, I'd gone with something that I thought was clever. As usual, my friends had managed to blow up my expectations in a way that was both loving and devastating.

"I still don't get it," Fox said. "Are you a sex kitten?"

They chose the exact moment when I was drinking some of Indira's hot chocolate, which meant all I could do for several minutes was choke.

West glanced over at me, gave me an appraising look, and said, "Dominatrix-cat."

"Oh my God," Fox said. "That's exactly it."

"It's hot," West told me. "You're totally going home with someone tonight."

"No," I managed to wheeze through death-by-hot-chocolate.

"What is a dominatrix-cat?" Indira asked.

"I'll look it up," Millie announced.

"No!" Fox and I managed at the same time.

"Aren't you just a black cat?" Millie asked. "I thought the keys just got stuck to you like that time you got wrapped up in all that tape in your office and you couldn't get it off and you kept shouting for somebody to come help and Keme laughed and took all those pictures."

"This is not like that!" I took a deep breath, which was hard since I was still recovering from my near-death experience. "And I would have been fine except Keme kept making it worse—"

"Well, what are you?" Indira asked. "Why don't you just tell us?"

"Because this costume is clever and original and—and insightful."

"Insightful?" Fox murmured.

"And I'm not going to demean myself and demean you and demean the whole human race—"

"He gets on that high horse quick," West said, "doesn't he?"

"You have no idea," Fox said.

"—by explaining it," I finished. "And why are you all so focused on me? This is about Deputy Bobby and Keme." I fought with myself, lost, and added, "And nobody even asked Fox about their costume."

"I'm a polymorphed dragon," Fox said—a tad haughtily, in my opinion.

No one seemed to know what to say to that.

Indira recovered first. "West, I've got thermoses here with more hot chocolate and coffee, depending on what the boys want. I brought blankets. And I've got dry clothes. Is there anything else they need for when they get out of the water?"

Shaking his head, West said, "That's perfect. What they really need is to go home, get in a hot shower, and eat something, but you need a crowbar to get Bobby away from his board, even at the end of the day."

"Babe," Deputy Bobby called from the barrier to the spectator zone. He had his wetsuit rolled down to his waist, and God help me, I looked. The world froze. Angels sang. Trumpets, uh, blew—it sounded better in my head. He made an impatient gesture, and for a disoriented heartbeat, I started to rise.

"Let me guess," West said as he got to his feet. "Zipper's stuck."

"Keme tried, but he can't get it."

West slipped under the barrier and moved behind Deputy Bobby to inspect the wetsuit's zipper. Meanwhile, Fox asked in a breathy whisper, "Good God, how much time does Deputy Delectable spend in the gym?"

"At least an hour every day," I said automatically—because ninety-nine percent of my brain was trying to commit every inch of Deputy Bobby to memory and, at the same time, pretend like I wasn't looking. "Usually before work, but same days he has to go after."

"Is that so?" Fox asked, and they turned a curious look on me.

The note in their voice made me flush, and I probably would have stammered something that made everything worse, but fortunately, Keme came to my rescue. He was jogging toward us, his dark hair up in a bun, and his face was alight with excitement.

"Keme!" Millie shouted and waved.

That poor, poor boy.

The word poleaxed comes to mind. I saw the instant he caught sight of Millie. And then it seemed like he couldn't see anything else. His eyes were locked on her (Millie was still waving of course), and Keme began to veer off course.

"Uh, Keme," I tried.

"Keme!" Indira shouted.

Fox stood and bellowed, "Hey!"

None of it helped, though. He couldn't hear us. And so he jogged straight into a rack of surfboards.

Keme went down.

The surfboards went down.

Lots of people started yelling.

"Oh my God," Millie said. "Keme, I'm coming!"

"You know what?" Fox said. "He might be embarrassed. Let him get himself together first."

Millie didn't look happy about that, but she stayed. Keme got himself upright, seemed to shake off the daze—although I noticed that he was careful not to look in our direction again, which was probably a mixture of caution and embarrassment. He got the rack upright and started returning the surfboards to their places. Other surfers joined him, but the initial shouting had died down, and it looked like everyone was in good enough spirits that the accident turned into something to laugh about, rather than cause for a genuine argument.

"There you go," West said. "All set."

Sure enough, Deputy Bobby had his wetsuit zipped up now. In case you're wondering, it was actually kind of worse, somehow. I mean, it fit him like a glove, and that's all I'm saying. He gave West a kiss, and West squirmed away, laughing, before he said, "You're getting me wet!"

"What's there to get wet?" Fox asked *sotto voce*. "He's got about six inches of fabric on him total."

I shushed Fox.

"Are you ready, Bobby?" Indira asked.

Deputy Bobby wore that huge, goofy grin. "Water's perfect—do you see those swells coming in? Perfect breaks today."

"I assume that means it's all good."

"The lineup is going to take forever." But his tone made it clear this was a small objection. Then, in a different voice, he said, "Oh, come on."

Farther up the beach, a group of guys had paused halfway through putting up another beach tent. Even with the tent only partially erected, it was easy to read the words spray-painted in red on the fabric: THIEVES and TRESPASSERS.

"What's that about?" I asked.

"A protester," Millie said.

We all looked at her.

"Keme told me," she said.

"Her name is Ali Rivas," Bobby said, "and she claims every inch of this coast is sacred land for various Native American tribes. She's been raising a ruckus for weeks. Vandalism, destruction of property, threats. Jen calls in something new almost every day, but nobody can prove this woman, Ali, is doing it."

"She strikes again," Fox said, eyeing the graffitied tent that the men were now in the process of taking down.

"Is this really sacred land?" I asked.

Millie shook her head. "Some of the tribes used to fish here, of course, but the only nearby ceremonial sites and burial grounds are on the headland."

We all looked at her. Again.

"Keme told me," she repeated, this time with a laugh. "And anyway, the Confederated Tribes are sponsoring the competition—they've got a tent down that way."

"That doesn't make any difference to her," Deputy Bobby said. "She said the leaders of the Confederated Tribes were sellouts."

"Yikes," Fox said.

Another man, accompanied by deputies, walked over to the vandalized tent. He was average height, heavyset, dressed in a polo and pleated khakis, and his hair and goatee were black as coal. It was hard to tell at a distance, but I thought maybe he was older—something about the way he moved. He said something to the deputies, who in turn said something to the men, who let the tent fall. The deputies spread the tent flat on the sand, clearly preparing to take pictures of the damage.

"Who's that?" Indira asked.

West dropped into his seat again. "Gerry Webb."

"How do you know that?" Deputy Bobby asked.

"Because he tried to pick me up last night," West answered. He adjusted the hardhat and gave a rakish grin. "While you were in the restroom."

Deputy Bobby looked like he might be thinking a few words you wouldn't find in most dictionaries.

"He's a real estate developer," West continued. "And he must be a good one, because the watch he was wearing cost over a hundred thousand dollars."

"He's the one that's building the planned community on the other side of Klikamuks," Millie said. "Do you know how much he's going to charge? A million dollars for a house. And that's not even one of the houses on the waterfront. And they're going to have a marina and a bunch of new restaurants and—"

"Wait, a marina?" Fox squinted. "Isn't the surf camp on the other side of Klikamuks? Gremlins and Gruntlings, or whatever it's called?"

"Gremlins and Grommets," Deputy Bobby said drily. "And yes, that's where it is. I don't know the details, but Jen said she worked something out with him."

"Who's Jen?" I asked.

Before Deputy Bobby could answer, Keme trotted up.

"Oh my God, Keme, are you all right?" Millie scrambled over to inspect him. She stood close to him. She touched him. She was wearing perfume. And God help that poor boy, he was wearing a wetsuit.

I gave Deputy Bobby a telepathic nudge and a meaningful look.

He almost laughed. "He's fine, Millie. We've got to get in the lineup, or we're going to miss the best sets." With a slap to Keme's shoulder, he added, "Come on," and then he headed down toward the water.

Keme detached himself from Millie as gracefully as a seventeen-year-old boy can.

We settled into our seats, enjoying coffee and hot chocolate and cake (cranberry upside-down) and cookies (pumpkin cheesecake, which yes, can be turned into a cookie). The wind picked up again, stiff with the brine and carrying a hint of surf wax and what I thought might have been recreational, uh, substances. A fair portion of that seemed to be coming from Fox. Once Deputy Bobby and Keme had their boots and hoods on, they collected their boards. Keme's gear looked piecemeal—probably assembled from castoffs or whatever he'd been able to score cheap. Deputy Bobby's on the other hand, looked expensive. It made me think of the rotation of expensive sneakers he liked to wear—another layer in the enigma that was Deputy Bobby.

True to Deputy Bobby's prediction, there were a lot of surfers waiting in the lineup. But it was a beautiful day, and the waves were plentiful, and we watched (and Millie cheered) as Deputy Bobby and Keme slowly worked their way forward.

"I'm kind of sad we'll miss it," West said.

I glanced over.

"The new development," he said. "It sounds like exactly what Hastings Rock needs—a breath of fresh air, new money, new people."

Because Bobby and West were moving; that's what he didn't have to say. West had told me they were moving. It had been one of the first things he'd said after he and Deputy Bobby had gotten engaged. They were moving to Portland. They were moving away.

"Are you sure you can help load the truck next week?" West's question broke through my thoughts. "Bobby said you don't mind, but I know it's a pain—"

"No. I mean, yes. I mean, I'll be happy to help. Do you need help packing?"

"We're almost done, actually. Thank God I was able to talk Bobby into using his leave—can you believe he wanted to work right up until we left?"

I could, in fact. Because not only was Deputy Bobby very good at his job, but he also loved his job. It was part of who he was. Or maybe just who I thought he was. I had a hard time picturing him away from Hastings Rock. What would he do in Portland? Who would he be?

West's silence jarred a response out of me: "Fox said they'd help too—"

"Absolutely not," Fox said without looking up from their phone.

"I'll help," Millie said. "Dash, we could make it a RACE! And we could see how many boxes we can carry at one time. AND we could see who can pick up the heaviest box! West, are you sad you're moving? Are your parents sad? Are you going to miss Hastings Rock? We're going to miss you SO much! I'm probably going to cry when you and Bobby drive away. Oh my God, I think I'm going to cry right NOW!"

Indira patted her on the shoulder. "I already told Bobby I'll bring sandwiches and sweet tea. It's going to be a long day. And I'll pack you something for the road, too."

"It's only a couple of hours," West said with a smile, but he patted Millie's shoulder as she wiped her eyes. "Hey, don't cry. We'll come back to visit all the time."

Millie sniffled and nodded and said, "And we'll come visit YOU!"

Maybe it was the sudden ear-blast, but West didn't look quite so happy about that prospect.

I almost said, *You don't have to move, and then nobody will have to visit anybody*, but my phone buzzed (and my better judgment got hold of me). My dad's name appeared on the screen. (Jonny Dane, the Talon Maverick series.) A call from my dad was—well, unusual was putting it politely. My dad's focus was on my mom's books, on his books, and on his guns, and not necessarily in that order. I answered.

"Hey Dad."

"Hey, Dashiell. How's it going?"

"Uh, good. How are you?"

"Good, good. Listen, I've got a great opportunity. St. Martin's asked me to edit an anthology—crime fiction geared toward men, you know? And I thought it'd be perfect for you."

"For me?"

"How's that story going, the one with the PI?"

He meant Will Gower, a character who had lived in my head for as long as I could remember. (That sounded better than calling him my imaginary friend.) In various incarnations, Will Gower had been a hard-nosed police officer, a hard-nosed FBI profiler, and a hard-nosed private investigator. He'd also been a Victorian bobby, a social worker, and a deckhand on an Alaskan shrimping boat—you get the idea.

"Uh, good?"

"Great, great. Send it over. We've got to get moving on this."

"Well, it's not quite, um, ready. A hundred percent, I mean."

Dad was silent.

"It's almost done," I said. "It's so close."

Millie patted my shoulder. Fox snorted offensively. Indira started unpacking one of the slices of cake.

"I can finish it up?" It was a miserable-sounding question. "Next week?"

"Dashiell," he finally said—and it held an unbearable amount of parental long-suffering.

Fortunately, at that moment Deputy Bobby and Keme started paddling out to catch the next set.

"Dad, I've got to go. I'll get you the story next week."

As I disconnected, Millie screamed, "GO BOBBY! GO KEME!" And then, without missing a beat, "Dash, that's so exciting you're almost done with your story!"

Fox snorted again. For someone who was, themself, an artist (and one who—I'd like to point out—spent a high proportion of their artistic time lying on the floor, moaning about how they were a fraud and a grifter and an untalented hack), Fox gave surprisingly little leeway when it came to things like, uh, purposefully postponing the day-to-day instances of artistic production. (That sounded better than procrastinating by goofing off with Keme.)

"Here you are, dear," Indira said as she passed me the cake she'd been preparing.

It was a surprise cake (meaning I didn't even know she'd made it—the best kind), some sort of gingerbread trifle. It was amazing, of course, and it went a long way toward taking the sting out of that conversation. My dad's silence. The way he'd said, *Dashiell*.

What helped more was that I got to watch Deputy Bobby catch his first wave. He made it look surprisingly easy when he popped up on his board, and even at that distance, I could see how natural he looked when he settled into his stance. He was actually kind of amazing—carving turns, slicing the water, his body leaning into each move until I was sure he'd fall. He didn't, though; he looked like he was glued to the board. I didn't know anything about surfing, but as far as I was concerned, it was incredible. And then, somehow, it got even better. Deputy Bobby launched himself off the lip of the wave. He went airborne, and as he flew above the water, he grabbed the back rail of the surfboard.

Millie screamed.

Fox shouted.

Indira shot to her feet, clapping.

West was jumping and waving his arms.

I was on my feet (I didn't remember that), bellowing Deputy Bobby's name.

It seemed like everybody else was cheering too, but I barely noticed. All my attention was on Deputy Bobby as he landed and rode the last of the wave toward shore.

And then it was Keme's turn. I recognized the look of furious concentration on Keme's face; every once in a while, I caught a glimpse of it when we were doing something else, when Keme forgot that he was supposed to be an unimpressed seventeen-year-old. His pop-up was a little less smooth than Deputy Bobby's, and it looked like he struggled, in the first few seconds, to keep himself upright. Then he caught his balance, and he seemed to change. The boy who vacillated between detached and surly (and occasionally outright combative) was gone, and in his place was a boy who looked...alive. That was the only word for it. It was like Keme was a house, and someone had turned on all the lights, and they were spilling out of him. He didn't have Deputy Bobby's finesse, not yet, but I thought, as I watched him carve the wave, that he might be more of a natural—if he kept surfing, he'd be better than Bobby one day; there was no doubt about that. But what made me grin until my face hurt was how happy Keme looked. How unselfconsciously at peace he seemed to be.

Like Deputy Bobby, he launched himself from the lip of the wave and caught air. Instead of reaching for the back rail of the board, though, Keme spun. He made it a hundred and eight degrees, but as he was coming back around, he smacked face-first into the water.

"OH NO!" (Guess who that was?)

Fox winced.

"Oh my," Indira said.

"God." West held finger and thumb an inch apart. "He was so close."

I went for supportive (mostly because I knew it would both gratify and annoy Keme): "Great job, Keme! Good try!"

Keme surfaced and shook his head. He paddled back toward shore. Bobby was waiting for him at the halfway point, and when Keme came up beside him, Deputy Bobby said something. Keme shook his head again. Deputy Bobby stretched over to give Keme a one-armed hug. When they separated, they paddled the rest of the way together.

"Aww," Millie said.

Indira patted West's arm. "That's a very nice young man you found for yourself."

"Yeah," West said with a smile. "He really is."

"Hugs are boring," Fox said. "I want to see them fight!"

A voice came over the speaker system, announcing that they needed the surfers to leave the water for the under eighteen division. In ones and twos, the surfers started making their way back to shore.

"Wait," I said. "Keme isn't eighteen. Was he competing in the adult division?"

"Obviously," Fox said.

"How?"

"He lied about his age," Millie said. "He does it all the time. When we go to the theater in Seaside, he pretends to be twelve."

"Hold on. One time—once!—I asked him if he had his driver's license, and he wouldn't talk to me for a week. I mean, he never talks to me, but this was...icier."

"Movie tickets are expensive," Fox said with a shrug.

I looked at Indira.

"I've told him I don't like it," Indira said. "But when you add a drink and popcorn, sometimes it costs us fifty dollars."

"I don't care about the movie ticket! I care about the injustice of him getting mad at me—"

"Babe!" West screamed. He ducked under the barrier to sprint the remaining distance to Deputy Bobby, who was making his way up the beach with Keme. "You were amazing!"

Kissing ensued. Lots of kissing. And while Deputy Bobby was looking particularly, um, estimable, what with the wetsuit and the salt-stiff hair and the general, uh, effect, I decided to look elsewhere. Out of politeness.

"I guess West isn't worried about getting wet anymore," Fox said with unnecessary smugness. "You know, I think it's a little unfair that Deputy Delicious looks even better somehow after being in the water."

"Fox," Indira said in a warning voice.

"Dash looks handsome after he gets out of the water," Millie said—with dubious accuracy but heartwarming loyalty.

"Remember after we went swimming, when we went to get something to eat, and the waitress thought he was a drifter and said he could earn some money washing dishes?" Fox said and began to laugh.

Indira said a little more loudly this time: "Fox."

"That was not my fault!" I said. "You stole my towel, and—no! I'm not getting into this again!"

By that point, fortunately, Deputy Bobby and West and Keme had joined us. Indira was pouring cups of hot coffee, and Deputy Bobby and Keme were shivering as they took theirs.

"You were amazing," I told Deputy Bobby. And then I heard what I'd said, and I rushed to add, "You too, Keme."

Keme glowered at me over the rim of his cup.

"I could have done it better, though," I said.

For a heartbeat, the glower cracked, and a hint of a smile showed through. Then he went back to that flat stare.

"I definitely wouldn't have fallen. Remember that part? At the end?"

His glare slipped again, but only for a moment, and then he made a very rude gesture.

"God, that was so good," Deputy Bobby said. "It's perfect out there."

"One day," West said, "when I'm a famous designer, we're going to buy a beach house. You'll be able to surf whenever you want."

He already can, I thought. Right now. Right here.

"You both need to eat something," Indira said. "Do you want to get out of those suits first—"

Before she could finish, a shout up the beach interrupted her. We all turned.

"You lying, cheating, thieving son of a—"

I recognized the speaker from around town. His name was Nate Hampton, and he was a used car salesman and member of Hastings Rock's city council. He was a lanky redhead who had chosen, for some reason known only to God, to wear a suit to the beach. And in that moment, he was charging at another man— the real estate developer, the one West had called Gerry. The redhead crashed into Gerry, and the men went down. They rolled across the sound, throwing wild punches that had neither force nor accuracy. It looked like a couple of pre-teens brawling rather than two grown men.

Deputy Bobby sprinted up the beach, and in a matter of moments, he separated the men. I jogged after him in case he needed help, but since he was Deputy Bobby, he didn't. The redhead was on his knees, wiping a smear of blood at the corner of his mouth. Gerry sat on the sand. He looked older up close, his face lined, but for some reason, he'd gone with pitch-black dye on his goatee and beard. Maybe he thought it made him look younger. In my opinion, it made him look like he'd fallen into the shoe polish.

"Mr. Hampton," Deputy Bobby said to the redhead. "What's going on here?"

"Nothing." The redhead got to his feet. He spat blood on the sand, leveled a furious look at Gerry, and shook his head. Then he took off toward the parking lot.

"Are you all right, sir?" Deputy Bobby asked as he helped Gerry to his feet.

"Fine, fine." But Gerry winced as he pressed a hand to his side.

"Let me get an on-duty deputy over here—"

"No need." Gerry detached himself from Deputy Bobby. People were still staring, and Gerry gave a weak wave. "We're all right here." He patted Deputy Bobby's arm. "Thank you, young man. Now, if you'll excuse me..."

"You should wait for a paramedic to have a look at you. We've got some chairs right over there."

"No, no, no. I'm fine." And with another of those limp waves, Gerry shuffled off toward the cluster of tents that marked the operations center for the surfing challenge.

"I'm going to make sure he's okay," Deputy Bobby said to me.

"Bobby!" West's voice had an unexpected edge as he joined us. "What are you doing?"

Deputy Bobby's face shut down. His gaze settled on something in the middle distance, not quite looking at West.

"The fight—" I began.

"Excuse us," West said to me.

I blinked and opened my mouth, but the only thing I could come up with was "Oh. Yeah. Sorry."

Deputy Bobby was still staring into the middle distance as I retreated.

"We talked about this," West said, his voice sharp and carrying over the crash of the waves. "You're not a deputy anymore. This isn't your responsibility. Your responsibility is your family."

Deputy Bobby said something too low for me to hear.

"What about somebody who's actually on duty?" West said. "Dairek was right there!"

Deputy Bobby spoke again.

When West answered, his voice softened. "What if you'd gotten hurt?"

Then I moved beyond the reach of their voices.

Back at the chairs, the Last Picks were waiting for me with universally miserable expressions. Millie looked like she was about to cry. Keme glared at me as though this were somehow my fault. Indira sighed and started unwrapping a sandwich. And Fox watched Bobby and West without the slightest attempt to hide their interest.

"That," they said, "is not good."

ACKNOWLEDGEMENTS

My deepest thanks go out to the following people (in reverse alphabetical order):

Wendy Wickett, for help with my repetitious phrasings (so many slumps!), for the great suggestion to distinguish fraternal / identical early in the text, and, of course, for her enthusiasm for italics!

Mark Wallace, for spotting my capitalization errors, fixing my italics, and as always, his insights into the characters (Keme, in particular).

Tray Stephenson, for his careful attention to plurals and possessives, for catching my weird typos (I have no idea what happened), and for his help with Olivia Newton-John!

Nichole Reeder, for her thoughtful corrections, for helping so much with continuity, and for even correcting my silliest stuff (the Von Trapps!).

Pepe, for asking the excellent suggestion about having Bobby follow Mason outside (even though, in the end, I wasn't able to use it), for asking so many good questions about continuity, and for helping me iron out Penny and Sharian's actions at the end.

Meredith Otto, for proofing the text, for keeping track of Bobby's description, and for being patient with my technical errors.

Cheryl Oakley, for her insight into Penny's search, for her questions about the paternity test, and for urging me to make the connections at the end stronger (which I hope I've done).

Ravkiran Mangat, for all her kind words about the prose, for asking so many good questions to get me to think carefully about the plot, and for her excellent suggestion that the tramp's corpse was perhaps not so cozy!

Raj Mangat, for reminding me about Dash's formal statement, for helping clarify the key details to the solution of this mystery, and for asking about the Class V haunted mansion.

Marie Lenglet, for all the ways she made this book better—with the mystery, with the characters, and with the text, all of which are better for her thoughtful analysis. And especially for the second read to weed out some remaining issues with the mystery and general story logic (the call from Cole!).

Austin Gwin, for checking my (sometimes made-up) words, for helping me tighten up the prose, and for his assistance—as always—with getting the details right for Fox's van!

Fritz, for catching my weird prepositions, for catching redundancies, and of course, for being absolutely right about mustard on a ham sandwich!

M. Winston Eisiminger, for help with continuity (windows!), clarity (dialogue!), and characters (Hugo, in particular, and his motives—or lack thereof).

Savannah Cordle, for all her kind words about Dash, for helping me fix the characters (and words) I swapped, and for wishing Dash would get shot (just a little bit).

Jolanta Benal, for her help proofing the book, including her willingness to accept (begrudgingly) "wainscotting," and her gentle reminder about redundancies!

And a special thanks to Alyssa, Crystal, and Raye for catching continuity and other errors in the ARC.

About the Author

For advanced access, exclusive content, limited-time promotions, and insider information, please sign up for my mailing list at **www.gregoryashe.com**.

Made in the USA
Middletown, DE
23 September 2024

61372687R00124